Dar Tania

*How the First Priestess of Tiamat Arose
and Founded the Dragon Empire Morbattania*

Look for these other great books coming soon!

Dar Tania, a 100 Page Story – October 2016
Malcor's Story – December 2016
Bomoki's Gate – April 2017
Syliri & Bruce – July 2017
Other 100 Page Stories – October 2017 on

For more information about the stories set in the Forsaken Isles, its characters, author, or whatever inspires you to contact Dar Malcor:

darmalcor.weebly.com

Library of Congress Control Number: 2016915383

Cover art by by Darko Tomic

Table of Contents

Author's Preface

I began playing fantasy games and reading fantasy/sci-fi with Tolkien's "The Hobbit" as an 8 year old. I loved it. Even loved the Rankin Bass 1970's cartoon about it, though it hurts to see that now. I can still sing "The Greatest Adventure" song from that animated movie. As I grew, I wrote and told stories, played various role playing games – you may notice elements from Dungeons & Dragons in my writing – and never stopped believing in a world of magic.

But, why magic? I often wondered what role magic and gods would play. It was never enough for me to tell a friend, "There's a dragon in the next room." I wondered why the dragon would be there in the first place. At one point, I began to study the mythology of dragons, magic, and approached religious studies with an eye to magic. I believe deeply in a world of magic. After all, we are the only animals on Earth that frivolously waste our time imagining. Given the choice of our sometimes bleak real world and magic imagined, I will choose magic every single time no matter how ridiculous it might seem or be.

If a dragon is in the next room, there better be a good reason for it! Welcome to the Forsaken Isles. This is the first book that sets the foundation for the dragon empire of Morbattania. It tells the story of Dar Tania, a young girl chosen by Tiamat to be her first priestess. My later works will focus on a period of time well after this one where people still know the dragons of Tiamat and the name Dar Tania has taken on legendary tones sung by bards across the realms.

Time flows in this world just like ours but to gods, immortals, and the endless, Time is poison etching away at their prime and bringing them closer to the end we all face. When Time started flowing, the eldar did not know what it was, except poison. Their reactions to it set the stage for our world, a shining gem in a sea of stars. You see, our world is in the exact center of creation, chaos, and warp. The river of time flows from this center towards oblivion. For those of us born into this world, our faith, our beliefs in the gods adds to whatever that god's dominion had been before Time. Our faith magnifies their power and adds to it. Sentient creatures believing in a god and choosing to act for that god can elevate that god above all others.

As you might imagine, this makes for a very dynamic pantheon. Long have the dragons waited for their first priestess. I give you – *Dar Tania*.

Special thanks to Tony Reynolds for serving as editor, and more thanks than I can express to my daughters who had to endure my frequent day dreams.

HEAVEN

CREATION

Dar

ABYSS
CHAOS

NAME

FLOWING TIME TO OBLIVION

ACTIVATION   SENTIENCE

Tania

HELL
WARP

How the First Priestess of Tiamat Arose
and Founded the Dragon Empire
~Morbattania~

Chapter 1 – The Goddess

Dar held her spear tightly to her chest. The forest stalked her. Dark branches and leaves hid the moonlight just enough to throw her off. Wispy clouds drifted high up but not enough to block out the stars. Though she knew the trails of her people well, no one had ever evaded their god. This test of her will and faith had played out many times in her life, though she had always watched it as a viewer. Being in it, now for real, with her heart racing, nothing could have prepared her for it, though every teen did this and talked about it after. Her test did not feel like her older friends' stories retold.

Somewhere behind her, the dragon totem presided over her tribe's bonfire vigil. They would be eating and drinking and telling stories of all the times they had almost survived. Their chief and his wife, the matriarch, would no doubt be interjecting odds of how long she would last and how or when the god would find her. She imagined the betting against her overwhelmed those thinking she would last very long. Still, she had lasted at least three hours longer than most.

This test could only end with her becoming a full tribe member, accepted as an adult. It always ended that way. The dragon god always captured his prey. Waiting for a cloud to help darken an opening ahead of her, she crouched and then ran as fast as she could. As she entered the clearing, she hurled a weighty stone to her side so that it would land and crash. She prayed the noise would distract the god even as she smirked, *No god would fall for this trick*.

She skidded to a stop into the roots of an ancient tree and calmed her heart. She felt the dragon move through the sky overhead, imaging the clouds breaking apart at his wings' touch. In this, its third passing, her arms and legs, and her neck hair tingled. Something in her primal and scared shook with fright. She felt it and breathed deeply. *Let it pass - please*, she prayed silently. The matriarch had warned her, "The serpent masks his power to protect us else we'd burn away in terror. When hunted, this fear leads him to you. Control that and you might just win, Dar."

She remembered asking how to control fear. The old woman had smiled, "There are more powerful things in the world than our fire god. Maybe one of those will help you. Against that terror, only faith and other powers can."

She prayed as the terror increased in the form of waves of pressure smashing into her with invisible force. Even the trees seemed to tremble. Then the ground shook as a creature of claws and fangs landed in the area where she had thrown the rock. Each wave of emotion sucked her into herself. When the god's tail unfurled and slithered around a tree just across from her, she felt her bowels loosen. *No no no*, she pled. It was considered the height of shame to be caught by one's own scent. She knew she was done for if something did not change.

Praying she touched the spearhead and threw it towards where the god's head must be. Halfway through its arc, the spear burst into fire. She sensed the dragon's massive body turn towards the spear. That was her moment. The tail moving ever so hypnotically through the forest nearby barely felt the pressure of her steps as she landed with a new prayer on her lips, but not to the fire god. Something answered her and strengthened her, guided her as she ran onto and then up the tail. The scales under her feet felt warm and almost like fur. She twitched her head, no distractions. Her prayers renewed as she ascended towards the growing spines. Only having seen the god from a distance, she could scarce believe how truly large he was.

A voice in her heart told her to run faster even as something held her balance on the moving surface. Finally sensing her, the dragon spun and crouched getting ready to leap into the sky. An uplift of warm air all around her caught in her lungs burning but she sprinted pushing herself faster. Only having made it halfway along the tail, she leapt the spines and continued her prayer, her inner conversation with that voice. That voice! It had become feminine, and, she felt, amused. It guided her. *Jump, grab the spine, duck right, call for strength in your legs* – and as she did, the god leapt into the sky. The force of its climb would have broken her legs, but bolstered by this new prayer, her legs remained steady, unaffected, and she continued to run.

Bursting above the trees into full moonlight, Dar saw the god's massive body stretching out before her. She felt she must reach the head. Continuing her race, the god climbed until the air became colder than she could imagine, yet the warmth of its own body saved her. Then, he stopped. The suddenness of his stopping caught her mid-leap and she continued to rise into the air. The voice begged, *what will you do child?*

She could only think of rope and as the thought formed in her mind, a thin coil of rope snaked out from her arms towards the dragon god. She had a brief moment of clarity as the clouds opened on the bonfire clearing below. She felt the matriarch's surprise as everyone turned to see the dragon god high above them. Too far away to see individuals, Dar turned back to focus as the rope stabbed out and tied to a horn spine rising up from the god's lower back.

"Beautiful," she heard the god breathe as his head turned and watched the line of magic wrap out from her hands. "Remarkable, little egg. Show me more!" His voice roared out with fire trickling from his jaws. The fear and terror smashed into her again but it seemed separate, somehow as if it

7

were affecting someone else. This separated feeling continued to grow and suddenly she found herself standing in the midst of a river of energy. Aware that she still dangled high up in the sky, this other part of her looked at the gossamer strands arcing from her hands into the swirling torrent of color. Something felt wrong though. She looked closer and saw her hands, her arms, disintegrating, eating away and flaking off. Strands of hair and shredded skin sloughed off in minute grains of time falling into that torrent.

"Lovely," the god's voice aired out over her and she looked up. The god stood entirely out of the flowing ribbon of energy. "That you see, that you are here with me. Stunning."

She could not take her eyes off the decay of her body. Watching, it made her stomach turn and she felt the beginning of nausea. "You are not in any danger, little one," a female voice said calmingly.

Behind the dragon god, the most beautiful woman Dar could have ever imagined stepped forward. Where her bare foot touched the river, it froze and she walked over it. The dragon god spoke saying, "This is my mother. Your goddess. The true power in the world. She is before Time. She is All. The mother of dragons. Your mother."

"I am Tiamat," the lady said. Tiamat sounded like her mother, like every mother she had ever heard. Looking at her, she fell in love, and then lust and a desire to submit and serve all warred in her heart. "You are the first to see me, human, to know me as Tiamat." This lady, who named herself Tiamat, looked back at the dragon god. "I never would have thought your plan would work, Alerius." Under Tiamat's half-praise, Dar saw the dragon god puff up with pleasure and pride.

Dar tried to say something but her face would not work. Tiamat leaned forward and offered her hand to Dar. Touching it, she felt her body explode with divine might and power as every part of her electrified and burned. The world around her, in this place, lit afire in a thousand colors. That female voice proclaimed, "Welcome Dar Tania, first of my priestesses. You shall care-take my throne, this gem, this world you call home - for it is mine. You will serve my children and bring me more like you. When you and I are in harmony, you shall hear my voice. Sometimes you may be compelled to take action, but for the most part, I desire your imagination and conviction. Pray and I shall hear your prayers."

High above, a ring of fire blew the clouds away. The tribe, watching with mouths agape as the mighty dragon god condensed into his human form and gently lowered from the sky, saw he cradled Dar in his arms. Stepping to the ground, the dragon god did something he rarely did. He spoke. "All hail Dar Tania – your daughter, first priestess of my mother Tiamat!"

The tribe fell to their knees and worshipped as the dragon carried their Dar into their circle and laid her at the feet of the chief and the matriarch. Each of his footsteps slagged the muddy ground, leaving a small circle of widening flame, but his heat did the people no harm. On that cold night, it warmed them. Alerius looked at them and then turned making eye contact with each of the leaders and sweeping over the tribe, he declared, "Hear me: the dragon totem is stricken. The time of the Goddess Tiamat is at hand. Tiamat is the one true god here. My mother. The mother of all dragons! Dar shall lead you in my mother's ways. The chieftainships' rule of the tribes is hereby stricken. The chief shall serve the Priestess and those she calls to her. Leadership of the soldiers will remain in the tribes, by my command." Behind the chief, the dragon totem carved of wood cindered and then blew away as ash. Across the tribal lands, everywhere such a totem stood, it also burned away. "Let your fastest runners go out and bring the chiefs, the matriarchs and the soldiers here. Now."

The chief made hand signs and immediately young warriors from the tribe ran forward and received a mark of paint on their foreheads by the matriarch. They sprinted out in all directions, and Alerius sat down on the dirt and watched Dar.

For six nights, the dragon god sat and watched Dar as she barely breathed. Chiefs, matriarchs, and soldiers arrived. Following the dragon god's example, the tribal leaders sat in meditation refusing food and water. Eventually, all arrived and waited. On the seventh dawn, as the sun crested the far eastern mountains by the sea, something trembled in the air. An excitement that rose in volume and then crashed to silence, over and over, until it was all they could do to remain sitting. All around, tens of thousands of birds leapt into the air as the dawn changed ringing in the colors of the dragons: red, blue, green, black, and white. Alerius opened his hands towards the sun and bowed his head. Everyone assembled did as well.

Walking in the sunlight, Tiamat appeared. Each saw her differently, felt her presence differently. She walked up and looked on them. They felt their lives unfold as if written on parchment and laid forth for her to see. When she smiled, their hearts leapt and visions of glory, power, and fame raced through them. She stopped above Dar and then knelt to kiss her lips. At her kiss, health flooded into Dar and for the first time since returning, color returned to her pale cheeks and then her dark brown, almost black hair, ignited into vibrant red. And, the Goddess left them.

Dar stood and took Alerius' hand. All around her, the tribes' mightiest had assembled. For her. Even this familiar dragon god. She felt the lingering glory of the Goddess. Feeling very small and insignificant, she found herself praying and then revelation and inspiration caught her tongue and words came, "Tribes of the dragon totem, long have we prayed waiting for a day when the dragons would choose us as their children. Long has the dragon god Alerius watched over us. The time has arrived that we must watch over ourselves and prove ourselves worthy of the name the dragons give us – children of the dragons.

"The goddess Tiamat has shown me in a vision where and how we are to come together and build an empire that will defy gods, overthrow tyrants, and shake the foundations of the world!"

She did not know where these words came from, and had never felt the power her voice held. Strong as her words seemed, inside she felt very much out of her element. Only the fire of the goddess' lips on her lips remained and it filled her with desire and lust and a thirst for action. Not knowing why, she called for a feast to be prepared. "After we eat, we will run to the holy place. Let word be sent to all tribes and all people to assemble at the foot of the dragon god's mountain at the holy place!"

At her words, some of the chieftains and the matriarchs leapt to take action and then caught themselves. The chieftain of her own tribe, the Horse, his face conflicted. All of their facial expressions belied their feelings, *who is this girl child to order us, let alone ALL the tribes?* That outside-herself feeling kicked in again and she pointed to the mightiest, the leader of the warg tribe, her finger pausing and then passing over her own chieftain. "Disobey the Goddess at your own peril." The ground around the chieftain began to glow as fire and ash lifted on waves of heat. At the last instant, Alerius caught the chieftain out of an eruption of divine fire. Everyone fell back.

Against the roaring tornado of flames, Alerius' voice spoke into their very centers. "You are each precious to me, but even I serve the Goddess. And you must too. You will learn it but for now, trust me. Dar speaks with the authority and blessing of Tiamat."

At his words, the camp burst into action.

Chapter 2 – The Temple At Morbatten

The matriarchs of the many tribes stood in a ring atop the large hill to the east of the dragon's mountain. Below them across the gently sloped valley floor, the tribes had gathered. All eyes focused on the young girl with shimmering red hair. Not much older than seventeen, at the Goddess' touch and the dragon god's affirmation, the young girl Dar now stood at the head of thousands of warriors, shamans, gatherers, and people of all ages.

The sun had crested the eastern mountains. Their dragon god Alerius landed just outside the ring. Rearing up on his hind legs, he spread his wings out over the northern face of the hill. An unassuming hunter, watching from the front of the gathering, stepped forward. The tribes murmured and whispered, asking *How dare he?* Suddenly all at once, the hunter's form burst asunder as his human skein fell apart and he took the form of another dragon. Like the dragon god Alerius, this one carried a weightiness of power but where their god burned, this one electrified. His wings spread just touching Alerius' wing on one side. While this happened, a small girl dressed in a simple frock with dirt on her face, walked up to Dar. Same as the hunter, she likewise shed her human form. The air around her crackled turning to ice that fell as snow. This one touched its wings to Alerius and the other making a triangle around the hill's crown. Dar raised her hand to catch a sun beam glinting in the falling snow, and began to pray to the Goddess for a holy place to worship, to serve, to train, to cherish, to protect, and to raise up the mighty empire from her vision.

The three dragons slowly exhaled their breath weapons into the prayer circle focused on that sunbeam. Painfully slow and achingly loud, a spear of ice and frost languidly reached down from the white dragon and touched Dar's hand. A moment later, an electric blue and green spear of lightning, and then a swirl of dancing flame combined. Dar prayed her voice turning over words from their dragon language into a melody that she somehow knew. From within her hand, a sphere of chaotic power full of fire, cold, and electricity pulsed and grew. The exhaled might of the three dragon patriarchs continued to feed into her hand.

Atop the hill and throughout the valley, waves of energy washed over the tribespeople making their hair stand on end and small children fall over. The witchdoctors and medicine ladies of the tribes standing around Dar prayed to the dragon god, and tried to pray to this new goddess. They felt something different but struggled to put words to it. The revelation that two other dragons gods had been with them warred in their thoughts and they struggled to understand how this could happen. Something in that feeling of confusion and mystery made their hearts leap for joy but it also taxed their spirits. One by one, they fell collapsing in place around Dar. Across the valley, one by one these tribal peoples gathered by the dragon Alerius collapsed. At last, only Dar remained standing held in place by the goddess' favor.

The chaos in her hand started to glow with the brightness of the sun when at last Dar heard the goddess in her mind proclaim, "Gently, place it to the ground. It is done."

Enwrapped by the dragon's breath weapons, Dar knelt and like planting a seedling, she lowered the writhing sphere of energy to the ground, and let it go. The dragons stopped. Time seemed to stop. That glowing fireball hissed and sizzled in the ground. Dar found she held her breath waiting for something miraculous to happen. Instead, the sphere hissed and absorbed into the ground. Nothing miraculous happened. Nothing stupendous occurred. Confused, she looked up at the red dragon patriarch. "I don't understand," she whispered.

"We are three of the patriarchs of dragonkind serving the goddess, the mother Tiamat. We must make this place sacred to Her. The vision you saw, we will build. The toil and faith of the people will make that vision reality. I cannot give you everything in that vision, or else it becomes just another miracle, just another thing that over the thousands of years of this empire, you humans will forget. I want it built by your hands Dar Tania. It will your first offering to the dragons and our Mother Tiamat.

"Long have I guided and protected this people. You Dar, your people are my children as surely as if you were born to me. In my vision, it is your faith and your sacrifice for this cause that makes you treasured and worth guarding. The other patriarchs will come later. We begin with Fire, Lightning, and Ice. Some of the patriarchs will come willingly. Others, we will bring, but all dragons – even the metallic ones - will find consecration in this place."

He reached out with a claw and stabbed it into the ground. The lightning and ice dragons did as well marking the corners of a very large triangle. Alerius proclaimed, "We will start with three obelisks here to mark the Court of Dragons. The rest of the vision will unfold as you rally the people into a mighty undertaking – the first temple to the Queen. Remember these words Dar, write them down. It is time there were a Book of Dragons."

In the hours that passed and as the people of the tribes lay unconscious, Alerius shared how he had selected her people some five thousand years ago to guide and forge into a nation. "But you were the first to hear Her Voice." The other two dragons spoke to her as well, sharing with Dar their impressions and thoughts as to how her people had grown.

The lightning dragon, who had an unpronounceable name, spoke most clearly. "Call me Spark," he said. "In the dawn of creation, you humans burned brightly and then your luster dimmed as other eldar experimented and reshaped you. Since then, you burn more slowly but Alerius has shown us the transcendent beauty and the possibilities of your and other mortal races. You have limitless potential. Each step taken to pull your ancestors closer to this truth has been painful for us to not interfere.

"Take something basic like water and swimming. We do not even notice water, well, except for the fire dragons who hate it. It matters nothing to us and so we barely consider it. But, for you humans, too much and you sicken and die, or drown. Too little and you wither, sicken and die. The right amount and you thrive, even playing in it. The ability to swim has proven time and again to multiply the odds of survival and expanded your people's abilities."

Spark chuckled, "And your children use it to play, in something so deadly!"

He paused and made a strange noise that reminded Dar of a thunder storm. She realized he was laughing. "Oh to see Alerius, mightiest of the fire breathers, trying to teach a human to swim! Though days are a just a blink to us, I'm sure those days felt an eternity!"

Alerius growled, "True and thank the Mother when they finally understood enough to start teaching their children generationally."

The ice dragon named Ynt'taris now spoke, "Step by step, not just Alerius but all of us have watched your people with fascination even during times when advances by other mortal races taxed our patience. I agree. It is time for you to impress us. Too long has it been the dragons watching over you, saving you from cold winters, famine, and sickness. It is time to build a Temple that even our Mother would be proud of."

Dar listened in fascination as the three patriarchs spoke. After some time, Alerius and then the other two returned to human forms and sat on the ground with her. She looked at Ynt'taris curiously, "You take the form of a human girl – why? I recognize you – "

"Yes, I walk amongst the peoples and watch. This form causes the least disruption and I have no wish to be a focus of worship. This form also elicits the most extreme of behavior amongst the tribes. Most receive it with empathy and care. Others with intent to harm. Through simple interactions, I have walked with the tribes and removed those who would harm innocent children. Their bloodlines ended."

The blue patriarch agreed, "Too much responsibility. I don't understand how Alerius waited this long. To dragons, treasure is precious and too many times, you humans recklessly endanger yourselves. The urge to intervene and fighting that urge is unpleasant. Plus, through the millennia, we have seen time and again how the most unpleasant and terrible of circumstance, creates great heroes. How do you do it?" Spark directed this last question to Alerius who sat armored in a burning halo of flames.

"Painful lessons learned over time. Humans increase their beauty and preciousness when they choose me of their own free will. Never before has a human shined so brightly as Dar when she heard the Mother's voice. You saw it. The desire to worship the divine is part of their makeup. And brothers, Dar you too, cast your eyes across all of our children and see, their faith and visions are rekindled. They burn like diamonds but more brilliantly than ever!"

Suddenly, Dar felt a shift and realized the dragons stared through her soul. Ynt'taris leaned forward and touched her face with cold fingers. "She is a treasure," the girl's approving whisper made Dar shiver with pleasure. The dragons, as one, turned to look out into the valley below. "They also shimmer with a light we have only rarely before seen in the chieftains, heroes, and medicine ladies."

"What do you see?" Dar asked.

Alerius touched her shoulder and suddenly, she stood in that place of dying again. "This is the River of Time, or what is also called the 'ethereal'. It is the flow of all creation into death and oblivion. We three were created before the River flowed. With the Mother's blessing, you will come to see, understand, and even use this for your purposes."

Dar looked around and, after recovering from her horror renewed at seeing her own decay, she noticed Lord Alerius burning brightly like a red star. Spark crackled with fierce ribbons of many-colored lightning. Ynt'taris stood as a small girl child behind which stood his titanic dragon form, translucent and pale white. It felt less exhausting to be here. "Behold yourself as we see you Dar," Alerius said and suddenly, from the river arose a phantasm of herself.

It glowed and sparked like a hot ember in a fire sometimes bright sometimes dim but always glowing. Alerius look upstream and called out in draconian and another phantom appeared. It was her but younger. It stood next to the first and she saw how small and tenuous the spark was from when she was maybe ten years old.

Spark breathed into the river lighting it with crackling power and said, "Remember the Goddess Dar, the Mother, how She called to you and ribbons of light reached out and held you to Alerius as you soared in the night sky…"

Remembering it and touched by the magic in his voice, Dar felt herself and the rush of cold wind along with that primal moment when she first heard the Goddess' voice. The first phantom, at her memory, blazed into life filling with multi-colored swirls of light. Spark continued, "Don't forget how it felt when you ran along his tail spikes and jumped, how your legs strengthened." Her aura burst outside of herself as the memory and the sacred feelings she had experienced came into her mind's eye.

"Your faith makes you glorious," Ynt'taris said. "By contrast, remember now something painful. We see them, you choose one and tell us in your own words but hurry, you aren't yet strong enough to endure this place for long."

Dar thought and the first thing that came to her mind, she spoke, "My mother died, when I was very young. She gave birth to a baby boy but neither she nor the boy survived. My father had died. It was just me as a little girl holding my mother's hand. I prayed but there was nothing. So cold outside. It was winter. My mother tried to tell me something. I had to pull my brother out. He was blue and weak, barely moving. I didn't know what to do. He died in my hands. His death hurt me. I wanted to somehow heal and save them. I'd have given anything to save them." Her voice had begun to shake as she told what she remembered. Here in this alien place with dragons forcing her to recall this memory she'd rather forget, it was too much.

Alerius, as she spoke, called upriver and this phantom scene from her past emerged. Shadowy and almost transparent, she saw herself and only part of her mother. Spark said, "Your memory is not strong enough for us to get more this many years away." Her younger self pawed at her mother's hand, her face showing pain as her mother's death convulsions pulled and crushed her small fingers. One last seizure and she held her baby brother with fear and hope, she tried to show her mother. Her mother was dead. The small phantom of light in her infant brother glowed dimly like a candle light flickering in wind. Her younger self sobbed holding her brother as that small light went out. Dar saw her younger phantom's aura too. With hope against hope, she prayed for her mother and then screamed for Alerius to help. "Please help my mother!" she had prayed. Her aura flared red hot during these painful moments and then all but went out when she had called and cried for her mother, for help, for anyone. And no one answered. Brief hope flickered with the baby brother's rigor mortis, and then darkness.

For long moments, there was nothing at all. Watching it all play out, Dar realized she had started to cry again. Alerius touched her radiating concern, "You did not give up hope though clearly you felt so scared and alone that you could also have died right there. Do you remember what happened next?"

Dar wiped tears from her face wishing the dragons would stop. Watching her tears age and blow away in the river, she nodded, "I walked out into the snow, to die." She felt Ynt'taris take her hand. "A small girl, lost in the forest –" she turned to Ynt'taris, "You? You found me. We went back and you helped me clean up and bury my mother and baby brother. You had a backpack and food. You stayed with me until the storm ended and the chieftain found us. I never realized it was you. Thank you Ynt'taris." Ynt'taris pulled her into a reassuring embrace.

All this played out in the phantoms very quickly. Hugging Ynt'taris now, her own aura exploded out of her heart in a shockwave of purple color and gratitude. "The dragons saved me. I never knew it."

"But you do now," Alerius said. "And you see for yourself why we find you so precious Dar. The first to see. Your time runs short. Look, quickly at this one." Alerius reached into the River and pulled up a chieftain, her chief, unconscious still. His aura smoldered red and black. "He resents missing out on what he thinks is a miracle." Alerius pointed to a cluster of dark-tinged red and green in his heart. "He is jealous and proud at the same time that someone so young as you in his tribe has gone from being just another child to command of all the tribes."

"And what am I exactly?" she asked as the River suddenly pulled at her cold and daunting. For just a moment, she saw the sparkling lights of her people, glimmering like rainbow diamonds in the plain all around them.

She opened her eyes in the real world. The three dragons stood opposite her and bowed. "You are the first priestess of Tiamat. We consecrate you in Her Name. So long as you honor this consecration and serve Her, you will progress in power and might forever." So saying, Alerius kissed her hair causing it to burst forth in crimson flames. Spark kissed her eyes causing them to turn sapphire blue. Ynt'taris kissed her hand and her skin turned porcelain smooth and white.

"These blessings shall mark all priestesses. We have faith you in you, Dar. Watch over my children," Alerius said pointing to the people all around.

"Draconian, my children is *morbatten* right my Lord?" Dar asked.

Alerius nodded. "Dar, be sure that you find time to write all of this in your own hand. The Book of Dragons has long awaited its prophet."

"I will my lord Alerius." She turned to look out over her people. They still lay unconscious. She remembered the radiant light of their auras. "If I may, why did you save me and let my mother and brother die? Were they not beautiful too?"

Ynt'taris took her hand and though in the real world the cold of it ached, it felt every bit as reassuring as it had in the ethereal. "We learned long ago that there is a fine balance between helping, like teaching the people to swim, and doing all things for all people. One creates independence, allows creative expansion of the soul. The other creates servants lacking in every way."

Alerius said, "In the beginning of the people, we did – I did – intervene in most things. That tribe called itself the Tribe of the Dragon. Though they were exactly as I liked, and though they were happy to be like that, they lost their luster when they began to see themselves as some kind of favored group, invulnerable because I would also intervene. They lost the ability to make good decisions. This lack of discernment led to their destruction. The tribal legends of the people are true, except they were not destroyed by a demon. I destroyed them. Since that day, I made a vow that I would teach, I would lead, I would exemplify. Not intervene."

Spark now spoke. "You, your mother, and the child Dar. You are all innocent. You are born into this world and do your best. In that struggle, the sacrifices and victories of your life make you precious to us. I want to tell you that we sent Ynt'taris to save you, because we knew the role you would play. The truth though is that Ynt'taris just happened, by accident to be there. It takes a civilization eons to evolve beyond base survivalism to divine acceptance. As the first, you will see in the matriarchs, that though they hear, they do not understand."

Ynt'taris gave her a hug. "It will be your decision as to whether you call on the Mother to save everyone or anyone or no one. Knowing what you know, knowing that you could have saved your mother, even your infant brother – would you?"

"Dar, you are exhausted. We will continue these discussions as often as you wish. The vision is paramount, but your training is our first priority for you in the days and years to come."

Chapter 3 – The Southern Concern

The knight Sean gripped his bastard sword tightly, sweating and trying not to look overly flustered. The King of Taysor sat high above him on a throne of white marble and gilded gold worked into the holy symbols of their god. The priest of Pha Rann, no – The Priest of Pha Rann Jeffreys Van, stood whispering to the king. Finally, the king looked to him and asked, "Sir Sean, where exactly is this messenger?"

"In the Shield Mountains south of us by what we call Winter's Cradle. She said she would wait for our return." The king nodded that he knew of the location. A popular camping and waypoint, the land formed a wind shelter there during blizzards.

The priest said, "She is going to wait all winter?" Sean nodded. "Is she protected?"

"No, well - yes. That is to say, we are not sure. I left a patrol nearby just in case. She could not have been much older than twenty years. She had this fiery hair. That is to say, her hair is red but it also burns with magical fire. She seemed unaffected by winter when I left her."

The king scratched his neck and asked, "And we have no record of any contacts like this from the Shield Mountains?"

Jeffreys, "No my king. We checked. There are some tribal peoples southward, but except for odd rumors of demon worshippers there, we have never had a request or an encounter like this."

"Is she even human?" the king wondered.

Sir Sean began to say something when the priest cut him off. "Only one way to tell but I would guess that you did not fight before coming back here. Am I correct?"

"Some of the zealots named her a winter witch and tried to attack – "

"What of them?" the king's curiosity spiked. The king headed on of the more zealous orders. Many of the knightly factions tried to outdo each other for their devotion and piety.

"The lady, she kept her eyes on me and ignored them. One of the zealots attacked but without defending herself or flinching, the zealot stopped just shy of cutting her."

"In your estimation Sean, were they right in stopping? What did you sense?" the king wanted to know.

"I felt a disruption about her, not good but if evil, not the evil I have come to associate with evil intent. Her intentions were not evil. Not with us anyway. I did not see it my place to prevent the zealots. Had they not stopped and we had engaged in combat, my sense is that it would have ended poorly for us." Sean added just as Jeffreys was about to pick up the conversation, "Her unflinching nature made me think that she knew the zealots would be unable to harm her."

"Interesting, but it's all speculation. Very good Sean," the priest said. "My king, we should invite her to court. If this is the beginning of a new thing, or a threat, it is best met here." The king seemed agreeable and so Jeffreys continued, "If she will not come, I'd like you to go with Sir Sean. See what I can learn."

A week later found Jeffreys Van waist deep in snow. Though the patrol had done a good job establishing camp, the continuous snowfall made travel difficult. They found the young lady had joined the camp and once they entered the perimeter of firelight, it seemed warmer. The troops were in a great mood and the priest immediately saw why. She was not just beautiful. She was beyond it. The odd color of her hair and eyes against that pale white skin was enchanting to say the least. Every part of her caught his eye at the same time and made him wish to throw himself at her feet.

The troops rushed to attention as they recognized the high priest, and the girl greeted them with a delightful smile. "Sir Sean, I see you return with a guest." At her words, the priest felt Sean straighten his back.

"Lady, may I introduce the High Priest Jeffreys Van of Taysor, chief prelate of Pha Rann? It is our custom to bow and show respect to the great sun god Pha Rann. Please bow."

"I am Dar Tania, the first and high priestess of Tiamat. Sir Sean, will Jeffreys Van be able to speak for your people?" She pointedly did not bow.

The priest urged his horse forward a step. "Sean, thank you. Dar Tania? Yes, I can. The king of Taysor wishes to invite you to our royal court. We'd like to learn more about you and this country you speak of."

Her eyes twinkled and Jeffreys felt something move in and around them through her regard. "You wish to understand if I and my empire are a threat you mean. Lucky for you, my ask is simple. Please, we prepared some stew anticipating your arrival today. Join me and let's talk."

The patrol broke ranks even though not dismissed to make food ready. Sean and the priest frowned. "Your men are overly enamored with her," the priest muttered to Sean who nodded.

The stew at least was excellent and Dar opened the conversation immediately. "I have joined the tribal peoples south of this mountain range together in a nation we have named Morbatten."

Jeffreys choked on a spoonful of stew. "You did this? Impossible."

"Not impossible. Nor did I do this alone. The dragons have allied themselves with us. Unlike ages past where your patrols would use their armor and swords against us, you will find that we have come a long way very quickly. I would like to invite you to our court. Granted, my court is but a tent in a valley but your country has things we need, that we will trade for. That we will buy."

"Ah, I see. You want our help."

"Possibly. Moreover, I want Taysor to recognize that this," and she pointed to either side, "is the boundary between our great nations. We do not desire to continue these off and on fights. I need my warriors for other purposes. I propose a trading relationship. I propose peace. I propose this mountain range as a natural border between our peoples."

Jeffreys felt that force moving just out of awareness all around them as she spoke and said, "If you're attempting to use magic to persuade me, not only will it not work, but I find it very offensive."

"No magic. I'm not a magic-user. I'm a priestess of the dragon goddess. You feel her spirit no doubt. It is not my intent to offend." She smiled and Jeffreys felt his mood and spirit lift.

"We will come and see Morbatten," Jeffreys said. "I must ask for the sake of my king, this peace offer and trading arrangement. They all sound good but does the rest of your 'nation' feel this way? Our records show these tribal barbarians to be demon worshippers and brutal savages."

Dar bristled a bit at that description and Jeffreys noted how some of Sean's men grew agitated at him. True to her word, no magic had been brought to bear. The men had not been charmed. They were in love. Jeffreys recognizes several zealots, and noted they too had fallen in love with her.

Dar took a deep breath. "*We* are NOT demon worshippers. You'll find and learn for yourselves that your demon stories are ignorant exaggerations of the red fire dragon Alerius, a powerful mage in his own right. Our hunters consider your armor and weapons superior to their own and would have wanted to take them as trophies. Our stories tell of equally brutal metal-wearing humans more apt to take prisoners and hostages than fight a fair fight let alone converse. I think you consider yourselves better than us." She smiled abruptly, "I look forward to changing that self-righteous attitude and proving that we can be brutal in war, but every bit as 'civilized' as your people. When trade is established, there will be no need for combat over swords and armor."

She turned and began walking south, the snow moving away from her feet. "We'll be ready for you in the first full moon of spring."

Watching her walk away into the snow, the patrol suddenly became aware of how cold it was. Jeffreys pulled his fur cloak more tightly about him grateful for the magic items that softened extreme weather. Sir Sean looked around and began barking orders to build up the fire and break camp, "Lets head back to Taysor and warmer weather in the next hour!" Watching his men, he turned to Jeffreys. "I hope that she was worth the trip?"

The priest nodded still staring at where she had walked away. "She has an endearing quality, even to the zealots. Tell me, these southern barbarians, what do you know of them?"

"Just the usual, that an occasional adventuring party would cross south and come back with tales of tribes bearing totems in the like of dragons, wolves, and other creatures, often embellished to look more frightening. Each tribe has a chief. Each chief has a medicine woman of sorts acting as an advisor. Some merchants attempted trade but for every success – and I hear they were fabulously profitable, there were several bad outcomes where everyone was killed or their goods raided and the caravan sent back with nothing. To be honest, my lord, this is my first time meeting one of them. I would have expected the pale complexions, dark eyes and hair, and strong but short peoples we have heard of. She was none of those things."

Jeffreys nodded feeling the temperature continue to drop. He could no longer see Dar through the onset of heavy snowfall.

Chapter 4 – The Spring Entourage

The Taysorian party had travelled westward around the Shield Mountains. Snow still lingered along any shadowed places. No doubt there would be at least one more snowfall before winter let go of the lower trails and roads. This particular road had been difficult. Sir Sean pulled his cloak over his face against the cold wind and looked at the road overgrown with trees. A branch whipped at his face and he swore. "*Road*. Bruce, your team abuses the word."

Ahead of him, the ranger captain shrugged. "It's a road to us. You'll get used to it. Besides this is nothing compared to that mountain range you scaled with me near the coast." Bruce referred to how they met. Sean, already a paladin known in the empire, had hired Bruce and two other rangers to guide him to a sea monster's lair. Getting there had been more difficult than fighting the monster.

"I doubt our Temple dignitaries and the prince feel the same way." They already had stopped too many times to help the wagon through mud and tangled undergrowth. The prince had a reputation for impatience.

Again, Bruce the ranger captain shrugged. "I'm told that whenever we encounter rough areas, the prince beats the driver. It's not my place to question the king –"

"So, do not question the king," Sean finished for him. "And pray for the best."

Sean found he enjoyed getting out of Taysor. Almost three weeks behind them on the road and soon they would be arriving in the southern valley Dar had indicated. Thinking of her made his heart leap while at the same time, he wondered about the ethics of his infatuation with her. With so large a group of priests, mages, rangers, guards, and servants for the royalty, they had seen but not been approached by any kind of raiders, thieves, or even monsters common to the Shield Mountains. It drove the zealots crazy to be ordered by Jeffrey Van to not give chase. Behind their group, several caravans of hopeful merchants struggled to keep up. Their mercenary guards, on high alert, had been well-paid for such a dangerous trip.

Bruce pointed as they came around a bend still high in the passes. To the south and rising high above the other mountains stood a single mountain covered in snow. Tendrils of ice blew from its peaks glistening white in the bright blue sky. "That is the dragon's mountain. Our destination is a valley just south of it. From here, if we cut east, we'll find a low lying and rugged valley. Huge. That's where the barbarians live. The dragon mountain and its foothills cut the barbarians off from the southern valley and plains. If you keep going south, you find hills, valleys, lakes. It's quite serene actually."

Sean took it all in for a while and tried to image a dragon circling that mountain. "Bruce," he said to the ranger, "what do you think of these barbarians uniting? And demon worship?"

That shrug again, "Taysor began much the same way. Well, if you go back to the Kinslayer Wars that brought our ancestors to these isles. We came here with our magic, our machines, our learning. These barbarians have not had that advantage. For them to come together, it reminds me of the Empire of One. If you go back in its history far enough, you find similar tribal beginnings uniting around warlords. Over time, they become empires. As to demon worship? They don't show the signs of it."

"Have you seen the dragon?" Sean asked.

Bruce nodded and with some prompting, he told his story. "Before I say, and because of our many years together, let me tell you something. The rangers know these are not demon worshippers. The truth is that the Order of Cuthbert came here once seeking demons and the dragon probably humiliated them. I know this because one of my earliest independent missions was to patrol beyond Taysor's borders and keep an eye out for any possible threats to our borders. The stories of demon cults here happen often enough, and I was young and stupid enough, to want to seek it out. I put together a small team and full of piss and dreams of glory, off we went. We didn't want to deal with barbarians so we took this road actually. The dragon's mountain is impassable on its north face. It's steep and icy almost all year long. Plus, the natives consider it and the northern valley there sacred. By sacred, I mean – hunt and kill you sacred. The southern tribes are more relaxed. So, we went the long way of this road to the southern valley.

"We entered the valley and carefully evaded the few tribes we encountered. They have totems headed by a dragon, embellished to make it more fearsome. See – demons? They have some agriculture in the valley as well though no permanent settlements. Eventually, we reached the base of the mountain. There's a crude trail that climbs the mountain. It's completely exposed so we went as fast and as quietly as we could. It took us two days to climb before we reached a large cavern. I expected to smell fire and brimstone. Instead, I only smelled rock and stone.

"The cave is huge. Huge enough for a dragon to fly through it. But, we were looking for a demon right? It's a straight shot to the center chamber. You know the dragons from our stories? The ones that sit on piles of treasure or lurk in dark places and torment heroes? This dragon is nothing like those. For one, his scales are dark grey veined by red veins that look more like mineral and less like a red dragon, though his body heat told us he's a fire-breather. And his size! I've heard stories of ancient dragons but this one would dwarf those ancients."

Sean asked, "You lived though so it was asleep I take it?"

Bruce laughed and rubbed his head, "Oh god no. The cavern slopes down towards his lair. We saw these glowing red disks once our eyes adjusted. We thought they were doorways or lights for the demon's temple. They were the dragon's eyes, glowing red. Each eye the size of a large wagon." He laughed again, "We had a priest. The priest called on Pha Rann for light and that was when we saw the dragon. Most of the group turned and ran away. There was this instinctive terror. You've heard about dragonterror right? Imagine that but so much worse. I just stood there paralyzed, unable to move. A part of me prayed the dragon was a statue or was asleep. It was so large and awesome. And that was when it happened."

Against Bruce's pause, Sean finally asked, "What happened? Tell me."

"It spoke. It said, "My how interesting. You came all this way to stand still and stare at me?" I didn't know what to do, I tried to say something brave and heroic. I think I squeaked and then finally told it I was looking for a demon. The dragon repeated that word and said, "I suppose it's all a matter of perspective. If you have come here to harm my children – the people you have been carefully avoiding, I would label you the demon and say you've found it so kill yourself."

Sean pulled up alongside Bruce to better hear. "I don't understand. That sounds like the dragon mocked you? I thought dragons were supposed to be vain and selfish, arrogant."

"I know! Me too right? And there were no children. No eggs. Nothing in my life had prepared me for that. Anyway, I sent a report to the temple. I'm sure you can find it. We talked and the dragon *let* me leave. Just like that. Well, he told me that if he detected my scent or the scent of my party on any of the people north of his mountain and they had come to harm, he would find and kill me, my family, and anyone in Taysor sharing my scent. And everyone else in my party. When he said it, I believed he would."

"Could a dragon do that?" Sean wondered. "I've heard they have amazing scent-detection but to follow it and find you in Taysor with its many tens of thousands of people. I wonder."

"I have no doubt of it, even now after all these years. That threat still haunts me in my nightmares. Sean? Listen. I have no doubt that the dragon already knows we are here and is watching us."

The trail, at a high point, came around a sharp bend and began a slow almost straight descent towards the valley at the mountain's southern base. They noted that the trees and underbrush had been cleared with some improvements made to the road itself. From here, the straight path moved towards a high foothill to the mountain's southeast. Bruce squinted and called for one of the elven rangers in his group. "Yes Captain, there is a large structure of rock and stone being built at the top of the hill. I also see what looks like a large tent city. No walls though."

At last they came down to a flat plateau fed by a spring. Tents dotted this and two guards with wolves on chains waved for them to stop. Bruce cautioned Sean against their brutish appearance. The guards asked a question in a guttural language they could not understand. One of them tried again in a different language but to no avail. At last, an older woman walking with a staff hobbled over. She bowed her head as if praying and then in perfect Taysorian asked, "Are you the group from Taysor our priestess told us to expect?"

Sean smiled, nodded, and dismounted. The wolves strained and the guards glared at him, but he bowed low to the woman. "We are. I am Sean, commander of this group. This is Captain Bruce. Though not here yet, we have some two hundred in our group. I ask for safe passage to meet with Dar Tania, at her express invitation."

The woman waved the guards and their wolves away. "She told us to expect you. I will walk with you. We are going to the Capitol." Eyeing Sean warily she added, "It's not a proper capitol yet but the Goddess has shown me. We all call it that now."

Following the woman, they made faster speed than they imagined possible. If anything, it seemed the road firmed under the old lady's feet and for them as well. In no time, they arrived at the tent city and then they came partially up the hill. Stair steps almost a hundred feet across had started to climb the hill towards the three large stone columns crowning the hill. Sean found his heart beating fast at the thought of seeing Dar again. He was not disappointed.

Chapter 5 – Stalemate

Dar waved at him from a distance and signaled him to come forward. A small dip in the hillside allowed for a natural amphitheater and Dar spoke to a group of what appeared to be veteran warriors and then women like their guide. She had grown even more striking in her appearance and radiated a calm sense of vision. Nearly scandalous in her lack of clothing last winter, her leathers had been replaced by almost sheer silks held to her legs, waist, and bosom by thin gold wire.

"I seek warriors able to hear the Mother's voice," Sean heard her say. "They will not necessarily be the strongest, mightiest, or even the largest. Though strong, they will have a wisdom about them. Though thirsting for combat they will also hunger for knowledge of this world and the works of her children. It may be one of you. You will each form into groups of three and a mother will go with you. I have a series of missions. It is my hope that through this quest you will advance Morbatten, and also find the Mother's Voice guiding you. You must report back before high summer or we will assume you have died with honor and another group will be sent to replace you."

She then proceeded to give scrolls of animal leather to the women. Some old, some younger, together they looked like a different race of humans from their male counterparts. Bruce noted it too, "They seem more alive and appealing. I don't want to say beautiful like the speaker," he observed. "More like they are easier on the eyes?"

Sean nodded. "Can you imagine if Taysor were like this? Dowdy men and desirable women? We'd be in very high demand my friend."

He heard Dar say to one, "We must find stone workers. We need dark grey stone, like these columns. They must reach into the heavens and be shaped however we wish. Find this stone and bring its location to me."

To another, she said, "Our Empire will consume all the food in this area unless we master agriculture. Find me those who can grow food and bring them to me."

As the squads took the scrolls and left, he and Bruce moved closer to her. To the last she said, "We seek the blessing of the god of this island. Search that god out and invite them to build a temple here that we may have a lasting relationship."

They waited till Dar had finished her business. "My lady," Sean said bowing. "You are radiant and beautiful. This is the captain of our guard."

He introduced Bruce. "We have another two hundred arriving behind us. I hope we arrived on time?"

Dar stepped forward and took his elbow, which sent shivers through him. "Your timing is perfect Captain Sean. Tell me, did the priest Jeffreys come?" She took Bruce's arm and turned them to look into the valley below.

"He did. Taysor's prince, second in line, Roland and his betrothed have come as well."

"Your words amuse me. These words like 'betrothed'. You mean they are to have children together?"

Sean and Bruce laughed as she led them up the remaining completed steps and then the switchback trail to the top of the hill. "We will build a temple to our goddess here, but I want you to look out and see Morbatten for what it is."

Sean immediately saw the rest of their group coming down from the plateau. It'd be several more hours before they reached the base of the hill. Bruce commented that it is a lovely view.

"I'd like to ask the Goddess to truth say you. I want to see what you see. I am so caught up in my vision of what it will be. I'd like you to see that vision."

Bruce shrugged that typical shrug, "I have no problem with it. I guess the captain will though."

Sean smiled, "I serve my own god. I cannot allow myself to come under the sway of another."

Dar pouted for just a moment. "You serve. Tell me, do you hear your god's voice?"

"I feel his light and guidance in my actions, especially when fighting great evil. I'm not sure that is the same as what you are asking. I'm a paladin, sworn to Pha Rann the great sun god. I live my life to oppose evil and protect this world for the greater good."

"I need to practice that," Dar said. "Being able to describe great purpose like that. It's very strong." She began singing softly in that different language and touched Bruce's cheek. "Tell me Bruce, look out and tell me what you see."

"I see a valley of mud and tents. A great mountain to the north. I stand on the top of a hill by ugly grey stone next to the most amazing woman I have ever encountered."

"Do you see anything when you look at the people? Tell me about them."

"I don't want to my lady. It is not kind," he said slowly the words struggling to come out as he resisted her truth spell. "I speak the truth at your coercion but do not wish to say these words."

"I need to hear it though."

He nodded. "My apologies in advance. The people of your nation are ugly and unappealing. You, some of the women who are like you I guess are different. The men, the people, the children… they are dirty. The language is unpleasant. There is a stench of human over everything here and I wonder if the dragon keeps you as food."

"Ouch," Sean whispered but he felt the same way and could tell Dar saw it.

"I see. Alerius told me you'd see it this way." She sighed. "I had hoped it would not be that bad. But, I have my own vision, let's see if I can't persuade you to see things differently. Right here will be a temple to Tiamat. It will stand forever. It will be tended by many of these 'amazing women'. The dragon's mountain will become the center of a powerful people able to shake the foundations of the world. The people below us, some will return to the northern plains. Most will stay and become the arms and legs of this empire. A great castle will stand on the plateau there where your prince, Roland, enters the valley. Dragons will crisscross the sky."

At her last sentence, Alerius burst out of the cavern and spread his wings in the sunshine as he dipped and then caught the wind and soared a lazy circle overhead. Sean almost fell to his knees as the dragonterror caught him. Bruce barely resisted. Dar touched them both and the feeling left. "We will be a people of dragons the like of which the world has never seen."

"You worship them?" Sean asked.

"No, we used to. He – Alerius – was the strongest on our totems. When his Mother Tiamat spoke to me, I learned many things. Alerius and a few like him survived the world's creation. Though like a god, he is not one nor does he wish to be treated as a god. He serves Tiamat, the Mother. He is the strongest of the fire-breathers. There are more. I reverence the Great Lord Alerius but I serve and worship the Mother. We are not food though Alerius has eaten criminals and others deserving of death throughout our history. But then, you can ask him yourself later today." She watched Alerius soaring against the perfect blue sky. "Why worship unknown, invisible, and unappreciative gods when they are right here with us? Your sun god shines on believers, non-believers, and the un-aligned the same."

Sean smirked, "Pha Rann created a perfect world full of light. Pha Rann's belief in his creations to resist evil and preserve creation, even against itself. I don't need to see divine servants to understand or commit to this cause."

"That's a wonderful way of looking at it," Dar smiled and took his hand. She pointed out over the valley. "Someday, this will be full of people and not just humans. I see elves, dwarves, halflings, minotaurs, civilized orcs, ogres, giants – all working alongside each other. It pains me though because I also see the rise of a great darkness, like a storm cloud full of black lightning and dire mist. I dream of a ram whose body rots away leaving only an evil skull behind and it whispers a name to me - "

Sean touched her lips, fascinated at how the fire in her lips sparked at his touch. "You dream of a demonic power. It has a name, but to speak its name gives it power. We call it the Jade God. It is the demon god of undead. Are you familiar with undead?"

"Do you mean those who rise up after death? There are some stories of it. We have stories of fighting against such."

The rest of the group was fast approaching the base of the hill and they turned to walk back. Not realizing how large the group from Taysor would be, Dar sent orders to clear a large part of the valley for them.

When at last Prince Roland's herald announced him, Dar stepped forward and welcomed him to Morbatten. He looked around, looked at her, looked around again, and sniffed the air. "I was told we'd be meeting a new nation. I see only primitives and barbarians. Who are you who dare speak to me?" The Princess walked up behind him with genuine curiosity in her eyes.

Dar took a deep breath. She had known this would be difficult. Alerius had told her it would be. "Most humans will see you as a desirable and beautiful trophy, but also as a girl. Remember, you are the first priestess of Tiamat. There has never before been one like you. Your actions will set the tone for all of my children."

Around her, her people muttered and she waved her hand to the side for silence. Praying in her heart, she found a core of strength. "Crown Prince Roland, so very nice to meet you and welcome to our great nation." She turned to draconian and prayed to the Mother as the ground around her grew warm and then ignited in a tornado of fire that arced up into the sky. From the middle of that funnel, she spoke, "I am Dar Tania, priestess of Tiamat and this new nation may be lacking in what passes for power in Taysor, but make no mistake, our unity and faith are all we need right now."

Roland stepped back as his bodyguard rushed forward with shields. Dar noticed that all bore the same insignia as Sean with only minor but consistent differences. She stepped forward and pressed her fire gently against their shields which turned hot. The paladins dropped them before they turned molten. "Power and good fortune to you Prince of Taysor." Magical shields appeared in place and the paladins pressed back on the fire. *Do not press them too far*, she felt the Queen's voice say. *Give them a taste of what they can expect if they do not cooperate with you.*

Dar raised her hand and called to the stones adorning the hill behind her. Her draconian words roaring out. From around them, Spark and Ynt'taris and then Alerius leapt and dragon-shifted to stand on the tops of those stones. The glory of their personages tinging the bright sunlight red, blue, and white. Alerius lifted his arms to the sun and around them, the stairs crackled and completed. The muddy ground underneath Dar and the entourage's feet solidified and flattened. Suddenly, from all around, sparks of red fire burst and tall armored giants flickered into view. The beginnings of dragonterror washed over the Taysorians. Curiously, the princess appeared utterly unaffected by any of it.

Dar locked her gaze with Roland, "Our faith protects us." She licked her lips seeing Roland's eyes struggle to not notice her sexual stance. Next to him, his fiancé pointed to the dragons.

The paladins guarding the prince spat back at her, "Illusions will get you nowhere, witch!" Swords burst into holy flames of yellow sunlight.

In that tense moment, Sean stepped between the royal guard and Dar, his arms outstretched as if to separate them. One hand rested on a sword point. The other burned in Dar's fire. "This is not illusion magic," he said. "Remember, we came here as their guests and they have asked for talks about trade. Surely this is counterproductive? My lord, Roland, let us retire to camp and, with this new information about their powerful allies, let us reconsider our plans? Time is our friend."

The royal guard paused waiting. Suddenly, Ynt'taris vanished from his stone tower and reappeared right in front of the prince and princess. The prince's guard stumbled backward as all the heat and tension seemed to vanish and transform into a terrible chill. "Tell me princess, would you like to see this nation from there?" The small girl form of the white dragon pointed to the top of the mountain and offered her hand to the prince's fiancé.

Princess Alaura looked at Sean and smiled. "She'll be safe?" Sean asked.

Nodding, Ynt'taris took her hand and jumped, dragonshifting into the sky.

Roland cast a dark look at Sean, one that promised retribution. "If anything happens to the princess – "

"She'll be safe or my life," Sean responded.

Jeffreys arrived at the front, walking as fast as he could. He frowned. "I didn't know dragons could shapeshift." He signaled for all to make camp. "A word with you, Captain Sean?"

Roland and the others went back to the wagons, which circled east to an open clearing in the valley. Jeffreys said, "You handled that well. I feared it would be too late to prevent the prince's guard from attacking."

Steps away, Dar watched Roland enter his wagon. He smiled and with a cruel expression in his face, blew her a kiss and then made an obscene gesture.

Sean caught the gesture but Jeffreys pressed for information about the people. Dar's fire vanished as explosively as it had appeared and she walked up the steps to the three stone obelisks. "Jeffreys, if I may suggest it. Have you ever met a dragon?" Sean pointed to where Alerius and Spark descended in human form to counsel with Dar.

Chapter 6 – Mischief

Sean pulled aside the tent door to Dar's tent and found her sitting on the ground cross-legged. She held her face in her hands. He saw her shoulders shaking and realized she sobbed silently. When he took a step towards her, all sound left and he understood. She had used her divine powers to blank the sound of her crying.

He stepped forward and tapped her foot with his boot. She looked up in alarm and tried to wipe her eyes and say something but her own magic prevented it. She began laughing and then cried some more. Sean smiled and sat back onto the ground trying to convey his friendly concern for her. Eventually, she recovered enough to end the silence.

"I look a mess," she said. "Sorry."

"The guards said I could come and convey a message from the prince. Had I known, had they known, I believe we'd have given you more time. You okay?"

Dar looked at him, "Why are you so different from the others?"

"My group, the paladins, we have different orders, or groups. My order considers itself pragmatists, that is, we seek the best course and embrace tolerance and differences so long as the greater good is being served. My group is very small. Most take a different course which is that Pha Rann's doctrine is absolute and can only be serviced absolutely, even for those who do not serve Pha Rann." He saw that his words helped and so he continued to describe the paladins. "We forsake wealth, personal relationships, and fame to serve because we have a vision, like yours, of a world that needs us. My people and its paladins are too quick to take offense. Over time, our culture has become pointed that way."

Dar stood and retrieved some tea, offering it to him. "Just a year ago, I was supposed to marry a chief's son. Not the eldest son mind you. I was not considered good enough to birth the next chief. The dragon god, Alerius, he tests us in a Coming of Age trial. Has for as long as our stories are told. Since my test, I've been this – " she pointed to herself – "and everything is different."

"What happened to the young man?"

"The chieftains squabble over who will marry me now. The only thing they can agree on is that any others are not good enough for me." She laughed. "They have never been so united. So I am alone in all this world, except for Alerius. Do you know how hard it is to go from worshipping your god to being friends with your god, and finding that while god-like, your god does not consider himself a god? I sound crazy to you."

Sean sipped the tea. "Not at all. He is your angel. It makes perfect sense that where the two of you share this dream, that you'd be friends. More so, imagine your loneliness but apply it to him. I heard you described as the first. We've had stories of a fire demon here for at least a thousand years. And you're his first. Think about that!"

Dar nodded, "It's true. He has told me that long has he waited for someone like me to come, who can hear and see and share in that vision."

"It is a good vision. Though I do not support your goddess' ultimate purpose, many lives will be better and uplifted through your vision."

Dar narrowed her eyes, "What do you mean – purpose?"

Sean looked at the tent entrance and the guards. "I'm not so sure this is the best place to have this conversation. I would also hazard you should hear this from your dragon friend Alerius."

She closed her eyes and after a moment opened them and said, "Alerius has invited you to ascend his mountain. Will you join me?" She fixed her hair, and something about her demeanor made her all the more appealing to him. Noticing his gaze, she smiled. "Trapped in the vision of a god, I was not ready for your prince to be so hostile."

Sean turned his head to the side and looked at anything else. He rarely regretted his vows, but everything with Dar and this place filled him with regret. "What? Now? The dragon wishes to meet with me now?"

"Yes, now. You were about to tell me the crown prince will not honor his invite for tonight with me and the chieftains. The prince has however agreed that his fiancé and others may. As such, Alerius has moved the meeting from the temple site to his throne chamber. Are all your princes like this?" When he did not answer, Dar insisted, "One of our children wanted to see a real prince. Roland kicked him in the face and threatened to kill him if he saw him again. Do you know what my people do to those who threaten children?"

They walked out of the tent in the rapidly chilling afternoon air. All around, her people worked with steady purpose. Sean noticed that all carried weapons and held a certain tension. Her guards walked with her to the base of the trail climbing up the mountain. Though night had fallen by the time they reached the path, the sky overhead provided plenty of light. Sean found that once he stepped onto the mountain, the air warmed and his step seemed eased somehow. Watching Dar's bare feet on the path, he saw the stone smoothing. When he asked, she shrugged it off as something that happens for all of them for as long as they could remember.

They reached the cavern entrance as the moon had begun lowering in the sky. Sean remembered Bruce's description of this taking two days. In human form, Alerius sat on a ledge hanging over space from the cavern. His view looked down into the southern valley. Torch, lantern, and magical lights glimmered and twinkled. "As a dragon, I cannot see fireflies. In this human form, the valley looks like a swarm of fireflies."

Sean thought Alerius spoke to him but the princess' answering startled him, "It is amazing, my lord."

She sat on the dragon's far side, her feet dangling over the edge too. She seemed totally relaxed and Sean wondered if magic had been used. He rushed to her side and found her safe, unharmed, and vividly awake. No magic seemed to enchant her. She pointed across the valley and told Sean to relax. "Roland said I could Captain. Ynt'taris and Alerius have been perfect hosts. The things I have seen! I never knew dragons were so fascinating!"

"I think the Prince's exact words were to question why you are gone for so long. Even with the messengers, it was a bit harrowing for him and the guard to hear you were "soaring the skies above the glaciers." Come now Princess, you are a royal but that is pushing boundaries."

Throughout this, Alerius did not move but he asked, "Is it so unnatural for your people to trust strangers?"

Sean chose his words carefully. "Strangers? Yes, by definition. It is always wise to be cautious. Also, you and the others are unlike any dragons we have ever encountered. And believe me, we have encountered many."

Alerius turned and looked at Sean. "You must mean you have encountered fallen dragons, or maybe you call them wild dragons."

"And what are you?"

From behind them, Dar spoke. "He is a dragon god, first son of Tiamat though the Queen has shown me that he and the others existed alongside Her in the dawn of creation. When the world first turned, when the gods fled this world, he chose to stay as her avatar in this world. As such, he is the patriarch of fire breathers. The other two are also patriarchs of their types. That is what and who Alerius is."

Sean stepped and turned to include Dar in his discussion with Alerius and the princess. "So, the white dragon we saw as a girl – Ynt'taris – is a patriarch of ice-breathers?"

Dar nodded. "Ynt'taris prefers that form. Says it is easier to walk amongst us."

"In Taysor, there is a mountain to our west, somewhat like this one, where a dragon lives. Many knights have gone there seeking fame and glory and came back with their memories wiped clean by magic and a phobia of that place."

Alerius laughed. "Yes, another patriarch resides there. The god of this isle granted some of us residence here when the world turned and the river first moved. Though that one came later as part of the Kinslayer Wars. I did not realize your metal dragon would choose to erase memories rather than coming out into plain sight."

Sean's face became alarmed, "A metal dragon? Oh, I see. A good dragon. That makes sense. None of the knights were ever harmed except for their memories. Though, the captain of our rangers said he once met you, Lord Alerius."

"Yes, I remembered his scent when you crossed into Morbatten. I never got his name but it is good he followed my cautions to leave my children alone. You wish to challenge my priestess' notion about good and evil though. You do realize that 'metal dragons' are no more different than colored dragons. We breathe the same weapons. We look and act the same. We have the same origin and lineage."

Sean smiled, "But color dragons are lent towards elementalism and chaos and are therefore more destructive in the mortal world. And of course, there is the matter of where your allegiance lies and the purpose of your god."

"Yes, so let's get right to it. Tiamat," Alerius said looking straight at Dar, "is the sole and truly rightful ruler of this world, which we call Tehra. She has claimed it as her throneplane. In genesis, it was the dragons that shaped this world. When the river began flowing, only a few like me chose to stay and endure its agonies. The rest left. There were two dragons mightier than all the others – Tiamat the Mother and Bahamut the All-Father. Bahamut was seduced by a group of eldar to leave this world and form a collective that would shepherd and watch over Pha Rann's creations." Alerius pointed to Sean, "This one and his people call that place Heaven. It is a nauseating place full of self-righteous spectators who have grown disconnected for what is real. They say, *Let's all work together and share the glory.* The truth is that there is no glory, only survival. The great survive and the weak fall. Pha Rann was part of the creation of this truth. Only when Tiamat returns can there be any truth other than this one."

Sean smiled, "I will not argue with the patriarch of fire-breathers, great one. I respect your view but would like to say a few words without angering you when Dar's instruction is complete."

Alerius' eyes narrowed to glowing red slits and he continued, "To remove themselves from the river of time, Bahamut said to us all to come and join him and share equally in the power and might of the dragons and the gods. Even amongst those who followed, there were some mightier than the others who said – I was one who said, "Why should I share in what is rightfully mine?" Tiamat then came and said, "Let them leave. This world we shaped is ours, we will stay and keep what has been earned, cherish that which has not yet been taken." Against that, I and my eldar brothers – we persuaded Mother Tiamat, the mightiest of the dragons, to leave Tehra lest the River diminish her, for Bahamut had already left.

"Of those who stayed, the reds, blues, and whites were most loyal to the Queen. Green, black, and the other colors had to be persuaded. We helped the Queen take a new throneplane as a staging realm for returning to this world when Time would no longer threaten her. From her throne, she watches over and guides us. The good captain here will most likely wish to note that her throneplane was carved out of what these humans call Hell.

"What the good captain fails to understand is that Tiamat has vanquished magnitudes more evil than all the powers of Heaven have. Removing yourself, regardless of the intent, from those you shepherd and protect is, in my view, selfish and short-sighted. Even an idiot shepherd knows that you watch your flock, with the flock – not from a distant tower. Heaven perpetuates a far greater evil than the assignation of Tiamat as a devil queen. On behalf of Tiamat and her dragons, I say to you Captain, your ignorance is offensive."

Sean felt a growing dragonterror as Alerius spoke and found himself trembling as did the princess who came over to his side and stood behind him. Alerius realized this and forced a smile. The terror receded immediately.

Sean took a deep breath feeling sweat crawling down his back and legs. "Well said. I would only add that, at least in our histories and teachings, to achieve a righteous outcome, righteous means must be employed. It is very clear even from what you have said that your purposes are an outcome that is not what Pha Rann intends, for a single god to claim and rule this world. This world is precious and unique."

"Because it is Tiamat's and she wishes it to be this way," Alerius interrupted.

"Because Pha Rann created it as a crucible for the free-willed to rise up and become gods themselves!"

Alerius smiled. "Though Tiamat was not the first, Pha Rann's creations were purposeless and devoid of free will until the dragons tested them with fire and shaped you all into this human form. Pha Rann did not create you Captain. The dragons did; I did. Humanity exists because of us. Ask your metal dragon if he created anything at all or if he just watched as the River poured out of creation and killed all in its path. You ascribe righteousness to the sheer act of creation when time and again, that creative force is twisted and ridiculed into monstrosities that threaten even Pha Rann himself."

Dar stepped between them. "My lord Alerius, Captain Sean, perhaps enough has been said. None of this shakes my faith. I welcome Tiamat's world. I am grateful to hear this exchange. It seems like I have much to learn."

The princess shivered and Alerius invited them into his cavern as wind from the top of the mountain blew ice crystals that fell like needles on them.

Chapter 7 – Under Threat

Roland glared at his fiancé, "You were out literally all day and night and you return smelling like dust and reptiles!"

The royal guard stoically pretended to not hear as the prince hurled invective at her. Alaura said, "I was learning so much! Coming here I was told, even you told me, to keep my eyes and ears open and to learn. Doesn't it matter that I did exactly that?"

"For an entire day? You could have been killed, or worse, magicked into some mannequin that would threaten delicate diplomacy – "

"You insulted their high priestess in front of her entire people yesterday!"

Roland squeaked and flew across the room to strike her but, one of the royal guards caught his hand, "My lord, one of the dragons has arrived."

At his words, the little girl child Ynt'taris walked into the tent. Her all-white eyes caught everyone frozen in time and ever so slowly, Roland forced his face to relax and turned his hand to pat the guard and say, "Well done, sir. Your gauntlet is in perfect condition." He stepped back. "Dragon Yen-tharis right?"

"Ynt'taris," the dragon corrected.

"Yes, well, what do you want?" Roland asked suspiciously.

"It is time. If you will follow me to the hill top, the high priestess would like to speak with you there."

Roland nodded and began calling for his things when, in a flash of cold and white, he teleported with Ynt'taris to the top of the hill. The three stone columns rose up a hundred feet above them and a stone table had been placed in the center. Ynt'taris leapt to the top of his stone, crouched down, and watched. Dar stood to Roland's side.

Dar waited for Roland to recover his bearings and then offered, "I do not want a war with Taysor. As you see, my nation is young. I would rather trade for things we need for the temple. It will enrich your nation."

Sniffing and covering his nose as he looked down into the valley, Roland replied, "I cannot possibly see what you people have to offer us in trade. How dare you kidnap me?!"

"You might be surprised. We have gold and other precious metals. We have magic and raw stuff to form magical items. We have our good will to offer."

"And you want, what – hygiene, food, wine?"

"I want artisans, stonemasons, builders, musicians, gem smiths, and mages. I need to teach my people these things. I want from Taysor freedom of travel, to open a road between our countries, to hire freely in Taysor for Morbatten's needs."

"No one from Taysor will wish to come here. It is all stink and sewage. You disgust me. Had I known it would be like this." Roland turned his back to her and blew his nose.

"You continue to insult when you do not realize something. You have a choice to be remembered as a great diplomat and negotiator, or as the one who made Morbatten Taysor's enemy. If Taysor will not satisfy my need, we will find it elsewhere."

"There is nowhere else," Roland scoffed.

"We will find it in the non-human races who hate Taysor."

He eyed her and said, "Taysor is loved the world over."

"No, Taysor is hated for its arrogance. It is coveted by the goblin nations and mocked by elf and dwarf alike. You speak of an ill-smell, yet you radiate conceit worse than your city's open sewers and unfed and unwashed poor. The worst of Morbatten is healthier and stronger than the well-to-do in Taysor."

"I have had enough witch," he spat the last word. "You invite us here under false pretenses, inflict indignity after indignity upon us, and now to my face you say these things?"

Dar signaled and from behind the stones, twelve chieftains stepped. Roland began screaming for help and Dar silenced him magically. "Taysor will not help us, however, there are those in the group who may. Return Roland, unharmed to his people. Ask for Sean, Bruce, Jeffreys, and the princess Alaura to join me."

The royal guard, which had began racing to the hill when their prince vanished, spotted Roland being carried, flailing and screaming down the hill, by the twelve chieftains. They rushed up to save him but found him writhing and twisting, cursing all manner of profanities, as the chieftains gently but firmly restrained and carried him down. Seeing the guard, they stopped and freed him. He stumbled into his guard, who caught him. "Slay them! Slay them all!"

The guard instinctively drew weapons and moved forward. In response, the chieftains – mighty warriors and hunters each – knelt and laid their weapons on the ground in front of them. One of the paladins just barely stopped his sword strike into the forehead of the nearest chieftain. With their prince screaming for war and death, the paladin met the chief's eyes. The chief looked old, wise, and did not flinch.

The moment stretched out and then Roland broke free of his guard and slammed the sword down into the chief's face. The paladin, realizing it too late, tried to resist. The magical blade sank through the chieftain's skull as gore blossomed outwards from the strike. Ripping the sword from the knight's hands, Roland spun striking at another chieftain who did not move, his gaze locked with the paladin's as if to say, "How can you allow this?"

Like his soul ripping free, the paladin called for the prince to stop as two more fell with throats torn and heads decapitated by his holy blade. The prince laughed maniacally as a magical ring on his finger slowed everyone else's movements. The rest of the guard sprang into action and finally caught and restrained the prince. Five of the twelve lay dead or dying. The remaining stood, retrieved their weapons calmly, and said, "We will continue. The high priestess asks for Bruce, Sean, Jeffreys, and the princess Alaura to meet her at noon."

Though brains and blood dripped down around them, the chieftains held themselves with more regal poise than a Taysorian king of legend. Behind them, the paladins struggled to restrain their prince who howled, "There will be war! How dare you treat me like this! Do you know who I am? What *you* have done?" Bruce and Sean arrived on horse to see the chieftains bow their heads and walk back up the hill. Nothing in their demeanor suggested violent intent, only sad resignation. Both Sean and Bruce had to help the guard drag Roland back to camp.

High above them, Dar watched and listened. Ynt'taris stood by her side lending vision and sound. "This is why Morbatten will never have a dynastic family. Alerius considered it but found that this behavior grows more common and threatening to the normal people, what he calls the Innocents, over time and by generation. Yours is the 200th generation that we have watched over Dar. Leadership will only ever be by merit here, same as the tribal chiefs; rule by the best not oldest or strongest."

"Roland threatens war over so small a thing?"

"So it seems. You are lucky his is not one of the paladins who serve Cuthbert. Though marked in what they call Heaven, Cuthbert sees goodness in terms of absolute. They are powerful fighters because they fight for absolute good. They are dangerous, very dangerous to you, if they decide that you are evil. Because Tiamat, as you now know, makes her throneplane in what used to be part of Hell itself, we are – no doubt – devil worshippers in their eyes."

"But that is not even close to being true."

Ynt'taris flinched when the sword struck down the first chieftain. "Come Dar, the surviving chieftains need you. You must heal them."

They walked down the hill together. The royal guard struggled to move Roland and keep him away from the people of Morbatten. The medicine women had arrived from the halfway camp and struggled to keep three of the five alive.

"I wonder," Dar said as she began praying in draconian. Her prayer became a song of health and revitalization. She touched the most sorely wounded chief. Immediately, his breath rushed into his lungs and the gash across his face and throat mended. The medicine women began to sing praising the goddess. At Dar's touch, the other two healed and she helped the last one stand.

Dar turned her attention to the first of the two who had died. She felt something in her prayer and wondered if she could restore their lives, but wondering it, her prayer lost its strength and she dropped to her knees exhausted, her hand resting on the chest of the decapitated man.

This, retold a thousand times, reached the Taysor entourage during a heated argument. From within a circle of his royal guard, Roland hollered and threatened that if anyone went to meet Dar it would result in a trial and conviction of treason. Jeffreys looked confused by the prince's behavior and did his best to ignore it. The captains Sean and Bruce stood to the side looking expectantly at the princess. As an aside, Bruce commented that it was too bad the prince had not fallen, but Sean elbowed him to shut up.

The time arrived where, if they were going to reach the hilltop by noon, they would need to leave. Sean stepped forward to take his leave. Roland silenced and glared at them with wild eyes. "Don't you dare – "

"I report to the Temple of Pha Rann. The head of my order, Lord Marshall Fuller, would love to hear why I passed up an opportunity to secure an alliance, or at the very least gather the maximum possible intelligence I can about this new presence on our southern border." Sean bowed.

Roland shrieked, "Jeffreys, you outrank all of the paladins, order him to not go!"

Jeffreys looked at Sean and back to the prince. "Alas my lord prince, the Captain's order does not fall into my own organization. I can ask but not require obedience in a civil matter like this." He looked at Sean and then said, "Sean, Captain, the crown prince Roland would like you to not go."

Sean bowed, "I understand. However, my conscience takes priority over royal liking."

The princess almost left with Sean, but only stopped on threat of divorce. Over his shoulder, Sean said, "While you may lose a royal marriage, there is nothing stopping you from joining us." He signaled for the ranger to join. A minute later, Princess Alaura burst into tears and ran out after them.

Chapter 8 – A Winter War

The three of them found Dar Tania sitting on the grassy hillside. The families of the two chieftains prepared their bodies for funeral. The priestess looked exhausted. When the princess saw the bodies and the blood drying in the grass, she shuddered and took Sean's arm. "I can't believe Roland did this in cold blood."

Sean replied, "The paladin who let his sword be taken will have a long atonement ahead of him."

Dar wondered, "And your prince, will he have an atonement?"

"I can only pray that the king metes out one, or that the prince reflects on his actions and seeks his own."

"That's a very catty way of saying that he will not be punished at all," Dar shot back. She tried to stand but was too exhausted from healing and the tension with the prince to do so, and fell back down. "Do you mind if we talk here?" The families had picked up the bodies and were walking away.

Bruce said, "A deal struck on the battlefield feels perfect for me. I commend your people's cool handling of this matter. Will Alerius kill Prince Roland?"

Dar pulled her fiery red hair back from her face in the wind. "Yes, as you would expect of a red dragon. Roland will die in a way that we'll remember for ages. I swear it on my life." The venom in her voice caught the Taysorans by surprise. Alaura touched her arm but Dar shook it off. "We invite your people here, basically to pay your entire country for help. We're not offering pelts or wood-carved trinkets! We're offering you the very currency your kingdom cares about!" She swore.

Sean sat down by her, noting how warm the ground and air around her had become. With ember light shining from her eyes and lips, Sean said with good humor, "It would seem that Tiamat's first priestess of fire has a fire in her heart too. It'll be okay," he said reassuringly.

"How?" Dar demanded. "Tell me how it'll be okay when Taysor sends a prince for peaceful trade talks and instead kills my chieftains – who command the fighters by the way; I don't yet command them – and declares war against us? What have we done to deserve this?"

Bruce and Alaura sat down by Dar. Alaura gave her a hug. "You've done nothing to deserve this," she said. "The Cuthberic knights, because you worship Tiamat, they view your nation as evil. Our king should have sent one of the Pragmatists, like Captain Sean."

"Alaura, you're going to marry Roland. Nothing you can say to me changes the original question."

"That's not fair," Alaura said. "I don't get to choose who I marry any more than you got to choose whether you worship Tiamat or not."

Alaura's words had a strange effect on Dar. She went stone still for a moment before she stood and looked at the three of them. "I think I see something now I did not before. You, all of you, even the people back in Taysor... you think we're some backwards tribal people full of superstition and ignorant ways, somehow that we're victims of the god emperor. You could not be more wrong." She pointed to the south and west. "For a hundred generations, when any of us disagreed with the totem, they left. They were not exiled. They were not killed or fed to the dragons."

Dar quietly lowered her voice and they heard her singing one of the many songs the Morbattanians had created around their daily lives. This one though reminded them of how Alerius talked and they did not understand the language. "I'm going to show you how wrong you are. You see," she spun back to them her hair, eyes, and lips burning with ruby fire. "You see, I choose Tiamat. And, Tiamat chose me. She has the side of Herself that guards and protects, like Alerius watching over Morbat." She lifted her arms to the sun overhead and began singing again.

Suddenly to their side, the ground twisted as rock spiked through the soil and fountain of clear water burst forth. Across from the gathering area, another fountain broke forth. With her right hand, she appeared to catch the sunlight and then she traced a symbol in the air. It hung there, heavy and gleaming. It pulsed and though they could not read it, they understood that it was a sacred symbol of Tiamat. "With this, I could compel actions of you each – crippling despair or make you believe every word I say. If I can compel you, Captain Sean, to break all your vows, why not compel Roland to peace?" Power came alive in her voice and she added, "I could do it, to all of you. You see, Tiamat's other aspect is the one where She rose up against the Consort Dragon and said she would not retreat from this world to the heavens. Takhissis, the fighter, the ruler of Tehra, the Mother of Dragons!"

Sean stood now and faced her. With pride and calm he confronted her anger. "You might be able to do these things. But, you won't."

The symbol of Takhissis hanging in the air before Sean pulsed from golden sunlight to ember red. Dar's anger hit them with heat. Bruce pulled Alaura back where Sean's armor and divine calling as a paladin protected him. Sean held out his hand, "You won't because we are not your enemy. Yes, there is a philosophy and followers of that, like Roland. But, Bruce, Alaura, I – I am not your enemy. Nor am I an enemy of Takhissis. Pha Rann knew your Tiamat and welcomed Her into the heavens. There is still love. Would you hurt those who love you?"

Dar's eyes met his, for just a moment, and the burning fire around her calmed just a bit. Sean continued, "By your own laws, Roland will be punished. By Taysor's laws, he will be punished. Would you punish us, Dar?"

What about trade discussions? I asked the prince for agreement that our peoples could travel freely between Taysor and Morbatten that we would repair and maintain the western road you came by. We need artisans, mages, and skills to be taught to my people. We excel in certain things but lack what we need to complete this great temple, and the education to be worthy of the empire I see in my vision. I suppose I must also add now that, the way of my people, the families and tribes of the two slain will most likely declare a vendetta against the prince. It would be good if your prince is gone from here today. Also, the dragons – they consider us, the people, to be their treasure. I cannot say how they are or will react to their treasure being killed. I do not want a vendetta by a few of us against a few of you to block what could be a very good arrangement for our nations. It is too bad that I have not been speaking with the three of you this whole time, though I see Jeffreys is noticeably absent."

"The priest and his order are headed by the prince's father. As such, he cannot leave the prince or disobey him in anything except an evil command."

Dar gestured at the blood-soaked grass. "You Taysors have blinders on when it comes to evil. Your prince relishes in the murder of – and you still serve like loyal dogs. I cannot imagine a "good" religion condoning such behavior amongst its leader class."

Sean and Bruce's faces darkened at her words. "I am no dog," Bruce snapped.

Alaura came around a bend in the hill. She had a backpack and looked like she had been crying. Seeing the blood stains in the grass, she shook her head, "I have never seen this part of Roland," Alaura said. "There are always a few stories, but to see it like this."

Dar, still angry, continued, "Explain to me how a prince murders five of my chieftains and yet it is the paladin who will be punished? Your so-called righteous god seems capricious and arbitrary to me. The goddess would never allow – "

Bruce tried to find an argument but standing in the blood of Roland's victims, he looked down ashamed. He shrugged, "Your goddess has a consistent vision of this world, that much is true."

"What has to happen to secure an agreement whereby Morbatten can recruit and hire skillful people to teach us how to build? Not just this temple, but other structures, roadways, and dams? I feel as if this is slipping away through my fingers and there is nothing I can do to avert war with Taysor."

Alaura sat down by her, "We'll find a way. I can think of several diplomatic ways to make this happen. My own family, though not as wealthy or powerful as Roland's, we have a lot of what you want."

Sean touched Dar's arm, "The prince is one of many. There are ways to bypass the normal process of a treaty. It is less formal but, if you work through the princess, you will find that you can get all you want."

"I want my people to learn," she snapped. "But without all this pointless murder."

Bruce sarcastically observed, "Your people are rife with stories of barbaric murder."

Dar met his gaze coolly and suddenly Bruce became aware of a presence looming over them from behind Dar. The presence resolved into the barely-there form of a human and had a divine presence to it. Bruce sought within his heart and realized, at the same time Sean did, that a messenger had arrived. Dar felt it too, but not the same way. For her, the presence carried alarm, and a sense of danger.

They dropped to their knees as Dar whirled. High overhead, the dragon king continued to circle the skies and they felt his regard. Looking more closely at the humanoid figure with golden bronze skin and white streaming hair, Dar felt a mix of fear, wonder, and excitement bordering on awe. Reminding her of when she first encountered the dragon Alerius, she noted the differences. The dragon had filled her with energy and vigor where this one invited her senses to calm thought if also high caution. She tried to make out if were a man but realized only its form seemed human. The rest of its features blurred to her eyes and she felt a blush across her skin as if sunburned.

"Great god Pha Rann, we thank thee for sending they angel. We pray thee, instruct us and share your wisdom. We are at a loss." Sean's formal prayer sounded appropriate and Dar became aware that they kneeled while she stood.

She considered kneeling but, at the thought of it, something strengthened her back and she lost herself in the overwhelming and all-powerful wash of power that came from the Mother's voice in her heart, "You shall not honor any other gods before me, child."

From her mouth, the Goddess spoke. "Your people stand in the way of my daughter's great vision and purpose. I counsel the Pha Rann to withdraw from my dominion."

The angelic being looked at Dar and seemed to smile. "We are not here to darken your children's hearts. The Pha Rann has asked me to intervene and ensure that Morbattania is prepared and ready for when the Mother of Nightmares arises up like a wave darkening even the night skies."

A part of Dar noticed how this way of talking seemed to mean something to Sean and Bruce. Her othervoice responded and she remembered Tiamat telling her that at times, she would be compelled to obey. Her voice said, "Tania must become every bit the military equal of and then surpass Taysor. My purposes are prevented by the murder of those who serve my priestess. I cannot –"

The angel made a gesture with its hand and the othervoice and energy left Dar. She collapsed to the ground choking, trying to hold her composure and failing. The being spoke, "The Pha Rann does not take orders, even from one of his mightiest creations. A day comes when even the night shall darken and the stars fall. Only a unity between Morbattania as the spearhead and Taysor as the shield will save this bright gem in the vastness of all creation."

The angel pointed to Sean, "The Pha Rann grants you what your heart desires paladin. You are to hold to your faith, but are released of your vows. So long as your faith endures, your gifts shall remain. Guide the dragons to their Queen and let us test them to see if they are able to forsake the darkness of Hell." It looked right at Dar. "You are the first to consecrate to the Tiamat. We see now." In a swirling of wind and warmth, the angel vanished leaving them in the cold autumn sun.

Dar blinked looking around. It had been achingly quiet and now sound and activity and nature crashed in on her. She tried to stand and almost collapsed had Ynt'taris not appeared at her side to catch her. The princess Alaura stood by the dragon. "What just happened?" Dar whispered.

Bruce and Sean spoke urgently and quietly to each other. Sean quickly answered, "You were, we were granted a vision. An angel from the shining god came to guide us. It is clear that the Queen's path is how we should proceed but first, we must move. Look." Down in the valley, Prince Roland had already assembled his train and had hastily begun to pull out leaving behind supplies, weapons, armor, even some of the wagons. Dar imagined he looked at her with hatred.

As her head cleared, she realized the messenger had brought them out of time entirely. She had some familiarity with the River, but this was different and she wondered if that difference came from the different dominions of Tiamat and Pha Rann. She made a note to question Alerius about it.

Chapter 9 – The Queen's Way

Alerius sat on his throne. As impressive as the great thrones of Taysor are, many having been brought from the antiquity of the Empire of One, Alerius' stood out not for its décor or flaunted wealth. It stood out because it emanated a presence of magic. Not just a seat, the throne had been enchanted ways obvious and subtle. Ynt'taris and Spark on either side looked at Sean impassively. It felt unnerving to have so many dragons looking at him. Bruce looked equally uncomfortable and it gave Sean reassurance. Alerius leaned forward, "The Queen's Way allows for commerce and humanitarian work across the borders, but leaves the door open for war? Do you have any idea how foolish this is for your government to allow? Had I understood this, my tribes would have attacked northwards millennia ago."

Sean shrugged, "It is an ancient tradition that is rarely used. Our histories show that many times, wars were ended when the people connected. This way allows for a human connection that can end war. There are rules. It is mortal on mortal combat. Other rules and conditions can be added if both sides agree, but it starts off as war, and then evolves as the vendetta burns out." Seeing Alerius about to question it, Sean continued, "There is a saying in Taysor that only the children's children forgive and become friends. In other words, the second generation is far enough from the vendetta to approach it with forgiveness, or at least peace."

Alerius laughed while the other two dragons maintained their blinkless stares. "Your people would trust this Queen's Way. Aren't you worried about retaliation? It is a point amongst my children to ALWAYS retaliate. We have no saying, though I have observed a similar second generation effect amongst my children."

Sean tried to bring his charisma to bear. "Great dragon king, times change. Ways change. Perhaps you should instruct your children to take a different view of vengeance? The angel described your people as the spearhead and mine as the shield. It was significant mighty king. You and I realize it. Your goddess surely does. But your people do not. Cannot new teachings be shared?"

Alerius sat back. "For millennia I have shaped this people. Inviolate in their beliefs is that new teachings come, but equally so is the principle of justice. There is no justice for the slain as they are dead. The mighty dead must have their day."

Bruce tried to speak but his voice came out as a cough before he cleared his throat. "Great dragons. What the paladin means to say is that you can have both. The Queen's Way only applies to warring states. Think of all that is accomplished by this. First," he held up his finger, "to acknowledge a declaration of war, Taysor acknowledges Morbatten. Second," next finger – "this allows the Queen's Way to be started. Third, your mighty dead will have their vengeance." Bruce started laughing. A burst of annoyance from the dragons that dropped him to his knees with dragonfear brought him back. He gasped out, "Apologies. Declare war against Roland. It's perfect."

Sean nodded. "It seems strategically sound. It accomplishes every objective. Though there will be war. A winter war. I recommend you limit the time of the war to winter."

Ynt'taris spoke and the girl's voice chilled them to their core. "And what of you paladin? The visitor's words to you caught our attention."

Sean blushed. "I, we… well, I would like to stay if I may have your permission to do so great dragons."

Ynt'taris stepped forward and ice shot from her steps towards them. "Why was a messenger required to give you this?" the white dragon asked from just a step away.

Sean began to shake with cold and tried to answer but his words froze in his throat. He kept trying to answer but at last, the words tore from him despite his best efforts to say something else. "Because I love her."

Alerius began to laugh. The white looked back at him annoyed. "You love her?" Sean nodded. "You have not been here long enough to love."

Alerius looked to Spark who, without changing his expression or taking his eyes off the two men said simply, "I do not see an issue with any of this. Love. Hate. Revenge. It does not matter how these humans feel, only that they execute the vision."

"I'm not done," Ynt'taris said to them. "So, an angel had to come and tell you it was okay to stay and love. Explain."

The cold withdrew so Sean could speak. "We swear an oath to the great god, to forsake these things. But I am just a man. I have never felt this way and I felt the great god pushing me towards my destiny. Only the great god can release me of a sacred oath."

Ynt'taris looked to Bruce, "And what about you? Have you too fallen in love with one of our daughters?"

Bruce tried to hide his smile. "No mighty one. My heart belongs to the wilds, the nightsky, and adventure. But this thing happening here is curious to me. If Sean stays, I will stay. I can't let one of our royals linger here alone."

Alerius said, "Enough Ynt'taris. Let this be decided. They may –"

"I want the winter war," the white stated. "All of it. It is mine."

Alerius nodded, "Very well, but when spring melts the snow from the western pass, your dominion ends."

"Yes."

Alerius nodded, "Good. Sean and Bruce, you may stay. Dar will be here soon. I can order her to be with you, Sean."

"No, her heart must choose. These things happening to her, they overwhelm her. She told me about her betrothal before her Coming of Age ceremony. The Queen Tiamat chose her. I would, of her own free will, choose me. I will stay as a servant to your vision." Sean bowed and for the first time since arriving here, both he and Bruce felt the regard of dragons and it elevated them.

"Yes," Alerius breathed. "The Queen's vision must cross all gods. But tell me paladin, if she chooses another? As the first priestess, I must have many children from her bloodline."

"I am a visitor in your lands, great patriarch of the fire breathers. I will stay and help forge this spearhead whether she loves me or not." These words pleased the dragons and though Ynt'taris came within inches of his eyes and glared at him, after a few moments, seemed satisfied and returned to his own throne.

Dar entered and bowed. Alerius said, "My precious Dar, there will be a war with the Taysorians. But do not worry. I foresee this war will never end. It will be a cold battle in the Shield Mountains that starts with snowfall and ends in the spring melt. Ynt'taris shall preside over this war. Let the families of those killed by the coward prince Roland know to ready themselves. Also," he gestured to Sean and Bruce. "These two have chosen to stay. I have invited them to stay as long as they wish. I hope this pleases you?"

Dar, without looking at the knights nodded her head and agreed. "I am glad for their help and perspective. I have struggled with how to approach the tasks ahead of me. Thank you." She then asked, "And this Queen's Way?"

Ynt'taris said, "It is already done. Alaura will stay with us a while, and then return to the coward prince bearing a declaration of war. She will also have a letter asking for humanitarian exchange. She is special to me. I will ensure this happens in the proper order."

"Men of Taysor, you are dismissed. Dar will find you tomorrow. Dar, stay." Alerius' words compelled them to leave. Watching them leave and waiting till their footfalls were no longer heard, Alerius said, "Dearest one, today has been a tough one. My children are not used to inaction when blood boils and battle calls. I am proud of you."

His words held and caressed Dar like a warm embrace. "Father, that prince. I do not understand these foreigners."

Alerius snorted. "Yet, you must. You heard the messenger and I have already recorded its words in the Book of Prophecy."

Dar looked at him and he explained, "You are the beginning. For thousands of years, I have watched over and guided your people to this, to you. I must step back as you step forward. All of this work, it is stronger when it is done by you, rather than me. It has to be about you choosing the Goddess, rather than a requirement or cultural thing. You'll need a book to share this time, these stories. There will be a book for each type of dragon, and a book for prophecies. You humans come alive when you are challenged. Giving everything to you makes you soft, like the Taysor people. Requiring and enforcing worship makes you sick in your heads like the dark elves and orcs. You are most powerful when you have a choice and make it with conviction.

"I have foreseen this and it is begun. When the time is right, I will entrust this book to your safe-keeping. Go and find Alaura. Bring her here." Alerius leaned forward and nudged her away. "The princess, Alaura, she is important to my brother."

Dar asked, "I have questions, god emperor." Seeing that Alerius would speak with her, she said. "Pha Rann sent an angel. Does Tiamat have angels?"

Alerius met her gaze and then softly answered. "Pha Rann must send angels because all of the eldar serving the Gate of Creation withdrew from Time to the heavens. Their departure marked the end of the Eldar. Without them here, Time, freely and without restriction, began to move though this world. I am Tiamat's avatar in this world as are those of us who chose to stay. My brothers, and many others. We chose to linger and suffer time's poison so that we would be here when you arrived, Dar."

"When they come here, the angels, they age? Yet, you are thousands of years old, if I understood your teachings. The way you talk about Time, it is hard for me to understand." Dar paused and then expressed, "The angels age when they are here. That must be it."

Alerius reached forward and touched her forehead. "You are correct. From a strictly "good" point of view, Time is a corruption of their Pha Rann created state. For some of them, they view Time itself as evil. So, they avoid it. But they are wrong."

"Teach me," Alerius begged.

"When I hunted you in the forest, during your test, what did you want?" Alerius asked. "Truthfully."

Dar said, "I wanted to do better than the Horse Tribe witch lady said I might. I suppose that, most of all, I did not want to humiliate myself."

Impassively and without expression, Alerius replied, "And, if we were to redo this test, how would it be *different*?" His eyes burst afire at the last word.

Without hesitation, Dar answered. "I would pray to Tiamat and I would find a way to win. I know I would win. I would be focused on what Tiamat wants, not humiliation or what an old lady told me."

"And, what brought you this difference in understanding?"

Dar thought about saying it was Alerius' teachings and more experience. At last, she whispered. "Time. I've learned. I had time to learn and take it all in. I'm a different person now. I'm a priestess."

An evil grin creased Alerius' face. "What magic is this then that takes a scared-of-humiliation little girl and turns her into a lioness that would beat the fire patriarch?"

It hit Dar, hard in that moment. "I'm not just different. I'm completely different. I see. You stayed to become different too!"

The god emperor's smile increased and with power dripping from his voice, he declared to her, ""Time is a weapon. Perhaps the ultimate one. The only one that matters."

Chapter 10 – The Princess Alaura

"You are so lucky to be so close to the dragons! This must be so exciting for you!" Alaura gushed at Dar. "Tell me about Ynt'taris. He, she, I'm not sure – she is so different than our stories about dragons! I must know more!"

Dar explained, "I do not really know Ynt'taris well. I don't know Alerius much either. It has all happened so quickly. It isn't like we ever sit down and just talk. All I know about the white dragon is that it prefers the small girl child form and someday soon I will have to face her as part of my progression as a priestess." She explained that a true priestess must exercise mastery in each dominion. "So far, I have only mastered fire and that thanks to Alerius' teaching."

They walked down the large tunnel into Alerius' throne chamber. Unlike other times when empty, the corridor stood now lined with giant sized armored statues. At first it had been off-putting as they both felt the giants watched them. Dar suspected them to be actual fire giants, but Alaura ignored them.

Entering the throne chamber, Alerius walked down to a table. On it sat a map of the entire island in minute detail. Dar touched it and felt it soft and furry. It was a tapestry. Noting her interest, the princess touched it too and Alerius said, "You'd be surprised how little escapes the eyes of a dragon." He moved his hand over it and the Shield Mountains came into view. He pointed to the south, "This is my mountain." He pointed out Taysor and its capitol, the coast, and the high passes connecting Morbatten to Taysor through the Shield.

"As you know Princess, our world is much larger than these islands." The map resolved to show a view of the entire world. "I have soared the skies around this world. It is all mapped."

Dar's eyes had grown wide as she saw how small their home lands were compared to the world. "We are just an island?"

Alaura gave her a reassuring hug, "A small continent actually, that tore itself apart in the Kinslayer Wars."

Alerius nods. "That is good enough. The truth is that the god of this world, Krentismar in draconian, granted refuge to survivors from what was once called the Western Lands continent. When that happened, I was already here though other dragons were not. I agreed to watch over a group of survivors now five thousand years ago. Cut off from what they once were, they lost their grounding and their faith. It has taken that long for a cleric to emerge from their bloodlines, Dar. You."

Alaura and Dar asked a few questions before Alaura said, "The paladin has explained the Queen's Way to me. I will do it but – "

Alerius finished for her, "You want to know more about Ynt'taris? I think my brother will agree."

From the shadows, the girl walked out. "Yes, I will go with Alaura to this Taysor. She will need help. Declaring war is a frightful thing." The girl smiled and the temperature around them plummeted.

Dar, used to feeling so sure of everything around the dragons, felt unsure. "So, we will fight Alaura's people? It seems like a waste to me. She is our friend."

"No," Alerius said. "It is a necessity. The people must make a choice – do they follow you? Do they seek vengeance? Do they want war? While it might seem obvious to us that they will want to fight, remember that everything changes. The forge of this world must turn." He looked Dar squarely in the eyes. "You must evolve into a high priestess worthy of a Temple. War will shape you into that, or break you. I hope not because I see such great things for you." Alerius looked at Alaura and added, "And yes, the princess is a friend of Morbatten. She has proven herself worthy of that title. However, the people of Roland's house, and those like Roland – to them, I say that we must show them our might and fury. Until we disabuse them of the notion that my children are backwards savages, Taysor will not take us seriously."

"My king, you do not know for certain?" Dar breathed into the silence of that moment.

"No, I do not know the course of your life. I am not the Goddess."

Alaura turned to Dar and said, "It will not be a war like you are thinking. Taysor has little interest in fighting when there is so much evil out there. Consider the paladin guards of Roland. They wish to be battling demons, not babysitting a spoiled prince. Their leadership tried to sway Roland to bring normal guards, but Roland insisted. Our paladins, those of the zealot orders, they quest out daily to find monsters. We have long avoided this land because adventurers either came back defeated by a shining warrior – that must have been you, great king Alerius – or they found only the barbarians, your people. They want more, to prove their holiness by conquering great evils."

Alerius chuckled, "Yes, even your ranger Bruce was one of those who met me. I have waited a very long time for this day Dar, Alaura. Everything must go well. Come let me show you something."

Turning, he walked towards the back wall of the massive cavern. It took a while to cover the distance and while they walked Alerius said, "I have carefully gathered together everything needed to create the spearhead the angel spoke of, though the Mother prefers to think of it as protecting and retaking what is already Her's rather than fighting off some demon force."

"The angel said the Mother of Nightmares," Dar noted.

Alerius nodded his head. "In the eldar times, as the Abyss formed, there were titan entities of such fearsome, if unfocused, will that they absorbed everything in their path. The dragons, I, we evolved to either fight or avoid such things. One of them, we named Set though in the mortal world, Set has become known as the Mother of All Nightmares. Even the Abyss feared it, and the layers of the Abyss are actually a prison to hold Set in eternal slumber. Sometimes, this world edges too close and Set dreams. From those nightmares spring forth monsters across the universe. Not all of creation is governed by Sean's naïve notion of Pha Rann. Even bound in sleep, Set spawns such terrible monsters that it would make mortals weep. Imagine should Set awake? We all see it – a day when the River flows black, and Set walks Tehra.

"But do not concern yourself with this Dar. It is far off and Morbatten and Taysor have eons to become the spear and shield. We must survive and thrive to that day, to stand and fight when even Time itself dies."

Reaching the back, he whispered softly in draconian and golden flames ignited around his hand and then outlined a door that had not been there before. This doorway led through a tunnel with many side branches. "My mountain is a fortress. Ynt'taris guards the top. Spark watches our borders. Though Taysor has not seen it, long have I known what is mine. Each of these side branches has something required to build Morbatten. Look." He pushed open a black metal door and from the burning light of his presence, the room beyond reflected back in pools of radiant gold and platinum. "There is enough here to destabilize every human nation that has ever been. I have many other hordes like this. Alaura, I show you this to know that even without me, Dar will be able to buy up any mercenaries needed to fight Taysor for centuries. I would suspect, to buy your own armies and turn them against you."

They continued past it with Ynt'taris occasionally speaking to add more information about library rooms, rooms full of armor, rooms full of weapons, and rooms full of grain. Finally, they came to a large door crisscrossed by red runes clawed into the door. Demonic faces moved and pulled at the door. To either side stood stone statues, gigantic in size, and poised for action. "This is my menagerie of nightmares. We, the dragons, have captured these here in stone for the training and education of my children. The door guards it should any break free. There is also a guardian. She is a medusa named Syliri, one who did not fall into the abyssal god of nightmare's, the one you call Set, dream." Dar looked curious but got scared when she saw Alaura's face go white.

"Don't worry princess. Like the kerchki, the fire giants, Syliri is every bit as much a child of this empire as the rest of my people. She is self-conscious. She was trapped by the River from her eldar state when Time first began to flow. She is my friend. Like you, she is beautiful beyond measure in my sight."

Ynt'taris nodded. "She visited me the other day and watched us, Alaura. She is looking forward to meeting you."

The giant door tore open like a knife cutting skin and tendon. The demon faces fled from the bleeding tear and then it was open. They walked in.

At first glance, the hallway they had been in continued but as her eyes adjusted, Dar noted that every so often, an alcove opened on either side. She eventually stopped and stepped into one of the alcoves. Braziers immediately burst into light and she recoiled as shadows leapt to the walls around her and a giant beast of eyes, fangs, and mouths appeared to lunge at her. "A mouther," Alerius said. "Spawn of Set and the Abyss."

A soft feminine voice with a faint hiss added, "All eyes and mouths and fury. This one had found its way into an iron mine and had started to feed on the Tribe of Fish."

From behind the mouther, a lithe female figure walked. Bangles and bracelets clinked together on her bare feet. As she stepped into the light with a sway, Dar saw that she wore a cowl over her head. Alaura saw it too, and then Dar remembered what Ynt'taris had said. Even the king had said it. She stepped forward and greeted her, "Syliri, I am Dar Tania. This is the…"

"Princess Alaura, yes. I know who you both are." She bowed to Alerius, but Dar caught her cowl and pulled it back. Though her hand flinched remembering Alaura's fear, she kept her face welcoming and smiling. Syliri's face of flat grey and faintly scaled skin framed gleaming purple-tinted eyes. Fanged teeth where a forked tongue flickered at her lazily. Except for that, her face was achingly beautiful. Not knowing why, Dar hugged her. Syliri flinched stiffly and then relaxed. Suddenly, what felt like a hundred snakes swarmed over her arms and around her face but she held the hug. "I like this one Alerius," Syliri said. "It is nice to not hide my nature."

Dar felt her hug back. Opening her eyes, she saw a viper inches from her. Though it feinted to strike at her, Dar met its eyes wondering if Syliri could see through the snakes' eyes. After a moment, the snakes calmed and randomly began tasting the air.

Ynt'taris spoke now, pointing down the hallway. "Over the centuries, as these nightmares have appeared, we have fought them to keep them far away from the children. Syliri petrifies them in the moment of their deaths. Even if they were to somehow break free. It would be only to die. Besides Syl, we have many other guardians. Just in case."

"And this passage is full of these statues?" Alaura questioned.

Syliri broke Dar's hug and stepped back. She seemed pleased and a faint color blushed her cheeks. "Yes. As we capture new ones, I create a place for them. You see, I served Alerius as an eldar. I serve him now still. When the River flowed, he saved me from those that saw only nightmares and brought me here. I worship the Goddess Tiamat and shall someday unite my dominion with Hers. Come, I have one in particular to show you."

Alaura walked up to her, a bit tentatively, and then matched her pace. "May I ask a question?"

Syliri inclined her head and, even though her hair vipers menaced Alaura, her tone of voice had a friendly bend to it. "You want to know if I am shape-shifted?"

"Well, yes. In Taysor, all stories about medusae are, um, they mention there are those who walk like you are, and then others – titans – who have a more snake like aspect."

Syliri reached her arm around both Dar and Alaura's. "It's not that we shapeshift. My sisters were trapped by Time in one or the other form. As you mortals began learning magic, mages started creating more or experimenting on them. They'd already fallen into Set's dream. Let me show you."

Behind them, Alerius and Ynt'taris both hissed, "Be careful, Syl."

Without warning, both Dar and Alaura found themselves caught up high above the cavern floor. While Syliri retained her upper humanoid form, her hair snakes elongated and thickened into tendrils reaching almost five paces down and around them and her body. Her lower body had become a snake's and it coiled back, past the dread lords into the darkness behind them. Faster than seemed possible, Syliri raced forward as her transformation powered her, shifting her arms into tough, almost stone-like claws. Her face, still flawless and perfect, had a more monstrous if serene character. "If Alerius had not saved me from Set's dream, I'd be trapped in either this or the other form. Look!" Her voice, heavy with lisping, opened her hands now, large enough for the two ladies to stand on.

All around, though they remained in Alerius' cavern, the very rock walls shifted and moved, crawling with worms. The floor, where they focused on it, burned away into deep vortexes full of razor teeth and grasping claws. The next alcove they came to held a petrified creature standing somewhat upright. Its body, all a mix of turtle-like torso and lower feet, extended into arms of bone spikes and hooks as long as a knight's lance. The head held voids where eyes should be. "I gouged its eyes out. It would otherwise see us, even petrified. We don't have a name for it. The fighters nicknamed it Hook Arm Monster." A parrot-like beak ringed by sharp quilled whiskers seemed to twitch at them.

Having noticed these things, the giant stone creature, like the floor and walls, began to cinder away into vortexes of energy. Syl's voice reassured them, "What you see is not real."

Abruptly, the stone shattered and the Hook Arm Monster lurched forward scything its hooks through the air at them. Dar and Alaura grabbed each other and screamed where the hook passed through them. "Set's dream, in this place, is all illusion. But, for the fallen, it's never-ending. Look at the dread lords behind us."

She swayed around. While the hook monster continued to attack them, seeking to wound and molest, Alerius and Ynt'taris morphed, enlarging into giant black fiends. Their magic armor did not, but around Alerius fire snakes erupted. "This is an illusion too. You are both loved. The dread lords would never hurt you."

The explosion of fire snakes lashed out at them oozing white venom. Just as they smashed into and through their forms and continued to attack Syliri, ice crystals that reflected their images warped and mutated lanced out into them. "This is enough," Alerius commanded.

Syliri returned them to the ground and shapeshifted back to her humanoid self. Alerius noted, "Set's dream is why you cannot really communicate with the monsters of Tehra. They do not experience the world the way the rest of us do. It compromises their ability to think, to choose, to be anything other than a fallen beast."

Ynt'taris said, "Syl, show them."

Passing the hook arm monster's alcove, they passed several more before they came to a large one. Inside this alcove, a gorgon every bit as large and terrible as Syliri had been reared forward. A strange-looking bow in her hands, the medusa's eyes gleamed at them even through its petrification. Her mouth open, fanged, and twisted by rage, Dar could feel its hatred of them. The leg-thick snakes had clustered into three groups. The ones around the face leered forward with that same odd gleam. "She was trying to petrify me when Syliri froze her," Ynt'taris said. "The other two groups of snakes were keeping an eye on Alerius and Spark."

Dar and Alaura, each tentatively, stepped forward and touched the lower snake body. "Alerius saved you, you said. How?" Alaura asked.

Syliri rose up, magically, to caress the face of her sister. As terrible and hateful the stone face was, Syl touched it with love. "Before Time, my kind were fascinated with love and other emotions. The ephemeral and fleeting nature of a universe full only of will and imagination meant that, if you wanted to appreciate and admire anything, you had to freeze it. We are tightly aligned with earth elementalism. Some of us petrified things, others paralyzed. The effect was the same. Our will froze the whatever," Syliri waved her to the side. "Whatever had caught our interest so we could study it. When Time first moved, all of the eldar tried to do something about it."

Syliri kissed the statue's cheek. "Someday, sister." She turned back and looked down and Dar and Alaura. "We tried to petrify Time. Obviously we failed. The harder we tried the more frustrated we became. And then, there was Set. Set twisted what we saw in time's flow and filled my sisters with dread and terror. It's all they see. It's all I see if I let myself. I fell into Set's dream until the god emperor freed me."

"Completing the first ascension rite, it grants a certain perspective and shifts the mortal one step closer to immortality," Alerius explained. "Immortality is so different from how the eldar were, I could not describe it to you in your lifetime. However, you might say that I killed Syliri and revived her in the ascension rite."

Alaura and Dar both nodded their heads listening. "Why not others then?" Alaura asked.

Alerius bowed his head and turned away from them. With a voice trembling and a rising torrent of dragonterror, Alerius said over his shoulder, "Syliri was not the first. Trying to help, I killed many of her sisters only to then have to slay them again in the first ascension rite." Ynt'taris put his hand on Alerius' shoulder.

Eyes wide now, Alaura understood. "Syliri was the first to succeed. You did not know if it would ever work."

Syliri nodded. "We were once numerous. As you might imagine, the eldar had a fascination for the universe. Taysor's stories tell that medusae are rare. The dragons killed many. The rest were driven by Set's nightmare away from the dragons." Syliri lowered to the ground and raced to Alerius. He turned to say something else, but she caught him in a hug. "I live in Tiamat's dream now."

They walked past all manner of horrors, great and small. At last, she stopped before an alcove and said, "This one is not dead, but trapped. It rages to break free but never will." She walked into the ring of light surrounding what appeared to be giant wolf. Unlike the others though, this one bore a sick green light in its eyes and Dar felt it regard her, with great hunger. Its flesh looked stretched, tearing free and exposing ligaments and tendons in spots, but its skeleton where showing crawled with runes burning with a green core.

Syliri pointed, "This is our enemy. Well, a general of our enemy." Alerius remained silent so she added, "One of the great hellhounds of the Necromancer."

Dar felt the creature's focus shift to Alaura, who suddenly jumped behind Ynt'taris. Ynt'taris' cold laughter echoed in the chamber as both he and Alerius stepped to the hellhound. Easily two men tall at its shoulder, its face had frozen in a rictus of pain and hatred. Ynt'taris trailed fingers along the hounds shield-sided paws leaving a frosty trail of ice and mist. Ever so subtly, Dar felt the hound's pain and rage increase. "This one entered Morbatten several thousand years ago and began feeding on the people. I captured this one in ice and Syliri handled the rest. We can't entirely kill it or hold it on the brink of death as it is undead."

Alerius eyed both the humans. "The hellhounds, their name for themselves, are free-willed servants of the Necromancer named Orcus. We do not say its name because unlike most other eldar, the Necromancer pays attention to and draws power from its name. It welcomes any chance to come to this world. I forbid you and my children from speaking its name though it must be taught so that it is not ignorantly used."

Dar's questioned whisper of "why?" so soft even she could not hear it was answered by Ynt'taris. "The Necromancer seeks to freeze all creation in undeath, static, never-changing, forever locked to the whim and will of that god. There is only one other god that holds such dire vision that all others unite against it."

Alaura said now, "Set, you named that one. In Taysor we call it Seth, the lord of horrors."

Alerius nodded, "Pay attention Dar. Set is the Mother of Nightmares. Before even the River flowed, the eldar noticed a mighty disturbance of one who spawned horrors and nightmares that fed on fear, pain, pleasure, and every other emotion to extremes. The monsters of this world, only a handful of which are in Syliri's collection, all come from Set. We united and bound Set in the Abyss. There it sleeps, dreaming, locked away from awakening."

"What happens if Set wakes up?" Dar breathed.

"The end, of everything," Alerius answered. "Unlike the Eldar, because of the River, we are divided and equally bound by new rules of causality. Even for gods outside of time's flow, there is a cause and effect that did not exist before time began. Set would blanket the universe in horrors. The river would run black as all creation falls into oblivion, even Set. Set claims oblivion as its dominion and believes that by sacrificing all of creation to it, Set will become the master of a new universe.

"Pathetically, there are humans and others who seek to awaken Set hoping for power and dominion in that dark universe. If Taysor were wise, it would focus on those. Tiamat's focus is on the Necromancer. Set is bound in prophecies so far in the future that we cannot contemplate it. But between now and then, there is the Necromancer. If we are to become a spearhead, the Necromancer is the anvil on which we shall be forged. Dar, as your faith and convictions grow, you will become able to harness undeath and use it, but you must be careful. Long have my brothers and I fought against the Necromancer. Long has it coveted revenge."

Alaura indicated she had a question and asked, "Why? I mean why fight and risk this? Taysor battles undeath but we do not have a singular mission to do so. There are those who openly study necromancy who also serve the cause of Good."

Alerius chortled, "The cause of Good. Princess, a day will come when you realize that there are many ways to achieve "goodness" in the world, and that some 'good' is merely misunderstood evil caused by lack of context and perspective. No 'good' comes from necromancy.

"Your people do it actively seeking out pockets of darkest evil and encouraging things you deem good, like feeding the poor and hungry.

Then, there is the Morbatten way. There are no poor and hungry here because I tend to them and have built a self-sustaining society by a moral code that prevents it. So Morbatten is and has been free of poverty and "the poor" since its inception. Alaura, Taysor's approach to the poor, as an example, perpetuates poverty. Your nation will always have poor and hungry because the systems by which your people feel they are helping, create a beggar class. Those inclined to naturally help, do not, because they choose to instead have faith in that system.

"Your use of necromancy, even my children's eventual use of necromancy, brings evil. Though I will not forbid necromancy, my children will be taught to recognize it for what it is, and to use it only when certain protections are in place. It will never be used on the innocents as it pulls them into the Necromancer's dominion. And I hate the Necromancer every bit as much as Tiamat does.

"Morbatten, I and the Mother, have chosen to resist the Necromancer. As the messenger said, we are to be a spearhead against it. Not a shield waiting for or guarding against attack, but the attacker." Alerius turned to regard the hellhound and grinned. "How many times have we pulled this one apart to learn its weak points? To learn about its connection and extent of its free will? It would make Taysor squirm. Yet, it is Morbatten who will cast off undeath while Taysor runs off into dark corners of the world looking for evil that is too distant to threaten anything that matters."

Chapter 11 – Morbatten Declares War against Prince Roland

Guards rushed to close the gates as paladins lined up in front of the drawbridge and portcullis. Down the street, a small girl walked towards them. The Princess Alaura trailed behind, walking between and side-stepping guards and warriors frozen in place in blue ice. Snow fell softly around the buildings in spite of the blue sky and blazing midday sun overhead.

The paladins held forth their holy symbols and prayed for immunity from magical attack and cold. Glowing in sun-yellow nimbus of light, the paladins charged as the fighters behind them secured the palace entrance. Ynt'taris welcomed the charge with a smile as, with the flicker of a hand, a wedge of ice filling the street froze into place before and then raced towards the paladins. Their divine protections failed to assist them as columns of blue ice swept their footing from frozen ground and then the column radiating from the small girl child slammed them back into the wall in a shatter of ice shards. Another sweep of her hands and a new lance of ice shot out to become a wall that slid along the ice and scooped the paladins into the moat. In spite of everything else freezing, the moat had only a thin layer of ice that broke and then caught, refreezing the paladins before they submerged.

The small girl, Ynt'taris – white dragon patriarch – and Alaura walked over the drawbridge as the portcullis made snapping and cracking sounds. Pointing to the paladins in the moat, Ynt'taris said, "I honor my pledge princess to not slay, unnecessarily." One of the paladins summoned his holy avenger and though it burst into flame and fire, Ynt'taris' hiss sucked the heat out of even that.

Through the bars, Alaura saw any number of retainers and guardsmen whom she knew well. She called out, "We do not wish to hurt any of you. Get out of our way!" Ynt'taris flicked the bars, which shattered at his entropic touch. All throughout the city district cries of alarm and drums built in tempo. Soon, the militia would arrive. Alaura felt sorry for them. She could also see how Ynt'taris selection of a small girl child played against the guards' morale.

In the moat, the paladins were struggling to move as the two passed into the courtyard. Immediately, a flight of arrows from all directions shot down towards them both. Ynt'taris hissed, "It seems your holy Roland and his zealot knights have little issue slaying you princess." From the little girl's form, a giant white wing unfolded and wrapped about them. A few of the arrows, magically-enchanted, pierced Ynt'taris' wing and draw a guttural moan from the dragon. And then came the terror. Having held it back all this time for the element of surprise, Ynt'taris grabbed Alaura and let all of his pain, hate, and rage for the eldar days now lost, all of his hunger and ambition for prey and lost might flow out from his heart. Alaura had felt a bit of this in Morbatten but never like this. In a circular wave, the terror pulsed out from Ynt'taris and seethed through the city. Drums fell silent and then mindless fear gave voice to cries of fright. Everyone in the courtyard except a few of the veteran soldiers dropped to the ground in fetal positions mostly unconscious but a few beating their chests and praying for mercy.

Those further away, turned and ran away from Roland's palace. In the distance, drums fell silent as shouts of panic rose up. Buoyed by Ynt'taris hand holding hers, the princess Alaura continued forward unopposed. The courtyard graced a large central entrance and climbing these stairs, they entered a large main foyer. Gilded doors large enough for a giant stood barred but at Ynt'taris touch, they shattered to snowy frost. Walking through, they found Roland hiding behind his throne. Only four guards, paladins Alaura recognized and knew well, stood between Ynt'taris and Prince Roland. They gripped their holy swords and prayed for divine aid.

Ynt'taris smirked, "The problem with divine aid is that it only protects you from direct magics and evil. What good does it do you against indirect and more tactical assaults, like this – " So saying, a lance of blue ice shot out and speared the throne. Roland fell back dodging the ice lance as the throne's wooden backing fragmented. Twisting like a serpent, the lance snapped taut and then Ynt'taris swung the lance and the entire throne side to side, battering the paladins away from the platform. Roland crab crawled back behind the stone foundation that had anchored the now absent throne. While the paladins struggled to stand and regain their footing on the increasingly slippery floor, Ynt'taris said, "The Princess Alaura is here to speak to her Prince. I recommend you stand down or I'll shed this human skein and bring the palace down around you. How many innocents need die for a message?"

Slowly, and with eyes questioning the Princess, the paladins resheathed their swords and stepped back. "It's okay," she reassured them. "I'm here to speak with Roland. Roland, come out from behind that so I can see you."

"Coward," Ynt'taris growled.

Roland looked out at them, clearly doing something behind the stone, and then stepped forward. He raised a crossbow knocked with a glowing bolt pointed unsteadily at Ynt'taris. "One move and I'll – I'll kill you dragon! This is a slayer bolt we made especially for devils like you!"

65

Alaura stepped in between the two and advanced speaking with each step. "We were sent on a diplomatic errand, by invitation to Morbatten. Your only job was to assess, learn, and bring information back to Taysor. Did you do this?" she asked rhetorically. "No, you insulted them and their ways. The dragons who watch over them, you offended at every opportunity. Their priestess, essentially their empress Dar Tania – you slaughtered her council of advisors with a stolen paladin's sword. As their emperor, the red dragon would say, 'You are a defiler of the innocent.' Their ways require restitution, or retribution. Will you not own your guilt to avert a larger war between Taysor and Morbatten?"

As she spoke, stopping a few steps from him, his face had gone from pale fright to the same livid anger they had seen on the temple mount. "I have no guilt," he said firing the bolt at Ynt'taris through the princess' chest. Ynt'taris dove forward to block the bolt, his girlish hand morphing into the skeletal dragon claws that would cover her from the attack. As if in slow motion, the bolt shot towards the princess. It had begun to glow white and tendrils of magic pulled it through the air towards Ynt'taris. Ynt'taris braced for the dragon slaying bolt's impact but then something happened.

A magical voice that sounded like the blue dragon patriarch Spark, intoned an otherworldly accent and phrase that resounded in the chamber, "Contingency to preserve Ynt'taris from a slayer."

In a heartbeat, Ynt'taris and Prince Roland magically transposed their positions, starring at each other. The bolt slipped just under the prince's crossbow and cracked through Roland' sternum. The dragon slayer bolt sensing prey that was not a dragon, went dormant but still pierced the prince's heart. Ynt'taris caught his dragon shift and returned to his human form, beaming at the Prince's death, holding the Prince Roland's gaze as the last life went out. "Die little prince!" she spat in his face. "Die and writhe into hell where your soul belongs!"

Alaura cried out, "No!" and caught Roland from behind as his body tensed and then began to slump into death's embrace. Ynt'taris eyed the knights, daring any of them to interfere.

"Princess, you must do it before he is truly dead," Ynt'taris reminded her.

Wiping tears from her eyes, she called out. "Witness! Roland, Morbatten declares war against you, until you are dead a 1,000 times." His eyes met her and his mouth twisted in a froth of blood and spit as he tried to answer and then passed.

"I loved you my prince," she whispered kissing his forehead. "I loved you with all my heart. But, what changed in you?"

Keeping his eye on the paladins, Ynt'taris said, "Only the gods can deal in absolutes. The eldar learned – painfully so – that the flow of time creates non-absolutes. It is a poison to mortals."

Behind them, the district militia began arriving. Seeing the girl of whom so many rumors had already spread, seeing the cowed paladins with their weapons ready but not brandished, and the prince dead with a holy Taysorian bolt through his chest, they came forward cautiously. Roland's guards stepped forward to intercept them advising caution.

Amidst the commotion, the district militia leader – a hero of great renown – demanded to know why, how, and what had happened. "The prince tried to kill the princess – " one of the guards started to answer.

Ynt'taris hissed loudly over their noise, "The Queen."

The knight continued, "The Queen, yes. The Queen Alaura is safe."

"And this?!" the knight said pointing to the girl Ynt'taris.

The paladin withered under both of their stares. "This is a powerful dragon and lord of Morbatten, a country to our south. We met them in our embassy there months ago."

Not standing down, the knight bowed to the Queen, "Many thanks for your safety my Queen. Alaura right? We met in the high court a little over a year ago if I remember correctly. My name is Thomeist, Imperial Captain. First Order. What is going on here?"

Alaura wiped a tear from her eye. "I stayed in Morbatten to avert war. I negotiated an agreement whereby Morbatten would leave Taysor out of its argument with Roland. We came here to deliver this message and I came here, to come home. Roland was going to kill me but somehow, the bolt intended for me, struck him."

The paladin guard said, "It was magic. Some kind of switching magic that changed their positions even as Roland aimed and shot at the dragon and her. Roland took the bolt instead."

Thomeist called for a healer to revive Roland but Ynt'taris cut him off. "No, reviving this one will expand war. For now, Morbatten is satisfied with the Queen's Way. I will take the prince back as proof to the families of those he murdered."

The knight frowned, "Murder? That is a heavy charge to lay at a dead man's feet. Are you sure –"

The paladins from Roland's entourage interjected, "The young girl, dragon, it speaks truth."

"I had heard of a holy sword taking the lives of barbarians. Isn't one of your paladins serving penance for this?" Thomeist asked, concern in his face.

Sensing things were calming down, Ynt'taris withdrew the dragonterror and sat down on the steps to the throne. Immediately, the sense of urgent panic and terror throughout the palace quieted. The dragon smiled at them making it easier to see the unassuming and non-threatening little girl sitting on the steps by Alaura.

"We'll just wait here until it is all sorted out," Ynt'taris said. "Roland is mine. The Queen Alaura is our friend and ally. The dragons are content with this outcome as are the tribes of Morbatten."

Chapter 12 – The Queen's Way Begins

Alaura gave Ynt'taris a tight hug, "I'll come visit. I promise!"

"Make sure that you do great Queen," the child said stepping back into the courtyard. All around, the Imperial family, the heads of the hundreds of knightly and paladin orders, and all around the city, thousands had gathered to catch a glimpse of the dragon. Looking to the king and the priest Jeffreys standing near, the small girl's body seemed to jump out of its skin as a slender and graceful if frightening white crystalline dragon appeared in the sunlight. Snow immediately began to fall. The dragon's eyes never left their mark.

Free of the girl's form, Ynt'taris spoke and though the terror remained in check, the ice in the dragon's voice and falling snow chased the almost-summer day's warmth away. "I speak to you great king of Taysor! So begins the Winter War between Morbatten and Roland's allies." Sweeping his head over the assembled peoples, he continued, "Be it known that my elder brother the god emperor Alerius watches over Morbatten. While I bring winter, he brings fire and ash. Doom. Nothing is to happen to the Queen Alaura. Your merchants and artisans are welcome in Morbatten with Alaura's blessing."

Raising his voice to a roar that sounded throughout the city, he spoke again, "For any who consider Roland a friend, an ally, or family. We will meet you in the Shield Mountains and hear your disagreement with swords. Congratulations! You are at war with Morbatten!"

Ynt'taris clutched the canvas-wrapped body still impaled by the bolt. One last look to Alaura and then the dragon jumped into the sky and opened his wings. The sunshine, snow, and light glinted through Ynt'taris body creating rainbow sparkles and a prismatic display of colors everywhere. The crowds watched until the dragon was no longer visible to the south and then returned to their daily lives. Small children began snow fights. It never snowed in the capitol. Except for Alaura and the king, all else in the great city of Taysor returned to normal.

In Roland's, now Alaura's palace, the king looked askance at her. "I sent an embassy and received a trade agreement, a declaration of war, and a hostile dragon has humiliated our great city. A white dragon no less. Remind me again how this is a good thing?"

"They are a people who love war and worship dragons my lord. But, they need our help. We can help them. Pha Rann even sent a celestial messenger to us to help guide. Because of that messenger, I came back here. The great hero and paladin Sean and the ranger Bruce chose to stay behind, with the Pha Rann's blessing. My lord, consider Roland. The people adored him. Even I was led astray from the darkness in his heart. I loved him since betrothal but never saw this in him."

One of the guards with the king snarled back at her, "Roland was a good man!" She noted they had trained in the same Imperial fraternity.

She kept her eyes on the king. "He seemed to be a good man but I saw him murder unarmed and non-hostile old men in Morbatten. With a holy sword! And he let the knight take the blame for it. Would a good man do this? Does a good man seek pointless war when even Pha Rann sees a role for this new southern nation?" The knight bristled at her words and stepped forward with clear intent to challenge her to swords.

The king cut the knight off, "Silence. The priests have confirmed that this is all true. I do not like that a Prince, and a highly regarded on too, did something like this. I suppose we owe you a debt of gratitude Alaura for revealing this viper in our midst. But then, you also terrorized the entire city and brought a demon dragon here. That beast kept us from speaking candidly. I'd like to hear this. Why did you bring a creature of pure evil into our city?"

Alaura bristled at the description of Ynt'taris as pure evil. "The dragon was concerned that Roland would attempt to silence me. It turns out to have been a valid concern. Ynt'taris is not evil nor a demon. Why do you name a creature that saved my life, averted war with us all, and was part of a Pha Rannic visitation as such?"

"You do not feel used or manipulated by any of this?" the ruler questioned.

Alaura shook her head no. "How could I? There was no manipulation. The only evil I saw in all of Morbatten was Roland."

He sighed and walked to Roland's throne and sat down. Though badly damaged, it had been reset on its dais. "Pardon an old man while I explain this to you. Please keep an open mind. You see, whether you like it or not, whether you see it or not, you are being used. And, whether I like it or not, you are now the widow of a prince and as royalty yourself, you are now a Queen. That puts your future children in line to our throne. So listen carefully.

"Dragons do not share. They do not have friends. Even the metallic dragons we consider divine and blessed are like this. It is not in their nature to have these human concerns. We are like insects to them. They can try and put themselves closer to our level, but at the end of the day, you are not the friend of a white dragon. You were a tool for a white dragon to come here and intimidate and demoralize our people. Morbatten used you to send a threat. I do not like that message."

Alaura's eyes had grown wide listening to him. "A message. Well, yes, a declaration of war is part of the Queen's Way."

"No, a message that if we do not agree to their unstated terms, they will bring war to us and destroy us."

From the entourage, a slender mage spoke with a voice like wind on a sunny day. "It's true Alaura. I have known Ynt'taris for a very long time. You no doubt believe yourselves friends, but you delude yourself. You are just a tool." The mage pulled back the hood to reveal golden orbs for eyes and silvery hair flowing down around a tanned face. "I am Oranstakar. I am a gold dragon. I balance the dragons to our south and serve as a secret advisor to the emperor's line."

All around, Alaura noticed that people had stopped moving, just like the messenger's visit. "My kind, we do not crave worship, respect, or the blunt crassness of threats like the Morbatten dragons do. We watch. Advise. And I know these things about Ynt'taris because I do not have friends either. Your lives come and go so quickly that I barely notice. The investment in 'getting to know you' is only worth it if I'm trying to shape generational outcomes, like Ynt'taris did by coming here with you. Already, the people talk about this day as special, scary, and different. The spectacle of a dragon flying off with a Taysorian prince and the fear that blanketed the city ensure that this story becomes legend."

Alaura shook her head no again. "They showed me. Alerius and the others, they see us as diamonds like the stars in the sky. No doubt we come and go quickly, but they showed me."

Oranstakar took her hand and Alaura noted how it felt warm and human and soft even though it appeared otherworldly. "Your heart wants to believe you are special, different, worthy of being the friend of dragons. Beware though child. Even to one like I, who dreams of Heaven, you are an amusement of the moment at best. To the dragons you deem friends, you are a cheap thrill."

Alaura suddenly felt as if her soul, her life, everything about her had been laid bare for this gold dragon to see. She blushed but steeled her resolve. Ynt'taris had told her this would be challenging. "I will take the Queen's Way. As Queen, I will ally with Morbatten and do my best to repair what could have been, what should have been a strong alliance."

"You play the part of pawn very well *Princess*," Oranstakar said as he walked away. Scant moments after he had departed, everyone else in the room and the district's noise came crashing in around them.

The emperor rubbed his temples and said, "That is the way of the metallic dragons my newest Queen. Our records show quite clearly that, though it may take generations to realize it, every dragon – good or evil – they reveal themselves to us only to use us. Even now, I am wondering at what purpose it must be that Oranstakar came to speak with us." He sighed and sat back, "Well, what's done is done. Tell me about the Queen's Way. They want a winter war with Roland's family. That is clear. They seem to want you to send artists and other skilled trade their way. What else?"

They spoke long into the night.

Chapter 13 – Trial of Paladins

"Not everyone is cut out to be a paladin," Sean said to the group of warriors. Unlike Taysor, he had been struck by the fact that, after word had gone out Dar sought skilled warriors, so many had shown up. Staring out across the field where they sat on dew damp grass, he counted several hundred men, women, and strikingly they were so different in their ages. "The balance to serve as a missionary, a holy warrior, a teacher, and a healer require not just that kind of personality but also inherent attributes that not everyone is born with. Though war-like, it is not a warrior mentality.

"Failure IS an option! Most of you do not have what it takes. I say this based on experience, not because I have any special insight into any of you. I commend your showing up to try."

One of the chieftains, an elder of many winters called out, "Your insight is blind then. MOST of us do have what it takes. Damn foreigner!"

It was a good-natured thing to say. Sean had quickly become known as the foreigner. Between the older ladies trying to marry him to their daughters and the men who saw him as competition for Dar, he had quickly adapted to being "the foreigner". He had already used that difference to smooth many an argument.

He waited for the laughter to quiet and then said, "It also takes a connection to the Goddess. You have heard Dar's teachings, shared in her sermons. When she speaks, you feel the Goddess. A paladin must be able to feel that connection at all times. That connection allows your god to guide, move, and assist you. Revelation can come at any time but obviously, during combat or during times of stress, it can be difficult to quiet your mind and recognize revelation in trying moments.

"This first test will show us those of you able to make that connection and feel your Goddess. Since I worship Pha Rann, Dar will be joining us. Until she arrives, you are to sit quietly and focus on the temple hill's three pillars. No moving, no speaking. If you speak, if you move, you are out. When Dar arrives, she will observe and may speak to you but until I release you from this meditation, you are to abide by these rules. Do you understand that if you move or speak, you are out?" Seeing their heads nod, he added, "You may stand, stretch, set yourselves in order. Prepare for this to last at least an hour. We will strike the gong three times, then two, then one time. Be here seated by the first gong."

When he finally struck the sound, even more people had come. He noted entire families with even small children seated and ready. The focus of these people astounded him. Many had shown up just for the chance of seeing if they could pass the first test. "No sound. No movement," he called out. Immediately, the grassy plains of Morbatten fell silent. Amazing.

That was at mid-morning. Shortly after high noon, he saw Dar walking towards them from the Temple. When she arrived a while later, most of the people were still there. "What is this I feel?" she asked Sean.

"It is worship and faith. Your people amaze me. Taysor has few people who can meditate for even a single hour. Every able-bodied Tanian – "

"Tanian?" she interrupted.

Sean winked at her. "Morbatten is a mouthful. Bruce and I felt that naming your people between Morbatten and your name would simplify things for the relationship with Taysor. Even in Taysor, we shorten it Sora, and call ourselves *Sorians.*"

"I see. Very well. *Tanians* – I like it." She smiled at him. "Tell me about this exercise."

"Bruce and I have counted 1,417 applicants for paladinhood. This meditation test is to remove those lacking the focus needed to serve as paladins. If they cannot retain focus in safe places like this, they will not be able to do it when their lives or mission is threatened. With you here, we are almost ready to begin the next test."

He went on to explain that the next test would be self-elimination. "The Goddess selects whom she selects. Using you as an example, the god emperor told me that he had tested your people for thousands of years before you proved able to hear the Goddess. This will be same but faster."

Raising his voice to address the entire group, he said, "A paladin is proud but also knows his limits. You cannot serve the Goddess and your own pride at the same time. I want all of you to turn your thoughts to your Goddess, to Dar Tania's vision of Morbatten. You are a proud people. You have powerful bodies and sharp minds. You have a history of survival and glory. These are tools for building your character, not who you actually are." He paused for a long time before stating, "You are children of dragons!"

He drew his sword, his holy avenger, and ignited it with Pha Rann's flames. "This is the hardest test you will ever face. Some of you will feel your Goddess' desire to serve. Some will feel her love but know in your heart that being a holy warrior is not your path. I caution you. With Dar here and the dragons watching, this is not a time for pride to convince you that you are something you are not destined to be. Know your own truth! Know who you are and know that you are loved and have a different path. Those of you not chosen by the Goddess, you may stand and leave as you receive your guidance. Do not disturb those around you and remember, no movement. No sound."

Moments passed and then more moments. From across the field, Bruce looked at Sean and shrugged. At last, an elderly couple marked by combat scars stood. They bowed to Dar and walked away. Some of the younger and ambitious fighters turned to see who it was. Immediately, Sean and Bruce pointed and signaled them out. Sean received many death threats that day.

By twilight, about half of the group had eliminated themselves. "I was expecting only a handful to remain Dar," Sean said. "So many still."

"What happens in Taysor when this occurs?"

"It hasn't. Ever. In Taysor, we only ever have a handful make it this far. I get the feeling your people will stay until they collapse. The number of children is shocking."

"Alerius has made it a point that children are to be educated and taught to survive and thrive. It begins with simple things like swimming, running, memorization games through song and games. As the child grows and expresses interest in things, they are moved from tribe to tribe to learn according to their interest. I'm not surprised at all that so many are here. Many of these boys and girls have already chosen to be warriors."

Bruce signaled and pointed their attention to a teen girl. She had not moved nor had spoken but a red light had begun to surround her. As they watched, other colors of lights appeared touching another thirty women. Dar looked at it all questioningly and heard the Goddess in her mind declare, "Behold daughter, your priestesses!"

"Sean, those glowing are meant to be priestesses like me." At her words, another handful were eliminated as the overly-curious looked around and then their eyes went wide to see the glowing auras.

By midnight, five hundred remained of all ages and the thirty one girls meant to be priestesses remained. At last, Sean called it. "Let their names be written in your holy book," Sean said. "Well done and welcome first paladins and priestesses of the Goddess! Return home, sleep, and rest. Join me back here in three days at dawn. Though you have passed, there will be a difference set between paladins fighting by revelation and those fighting by skill and cunning, which we call knights. Both are holy warriors and both have their destinies and roles set by martial cunning or divine inspiration. Come with armor and weapons, food and drink, and whatever other support you require for days of training, fighting, and perhaps even death."

The days that followed passed in a blur of preparations. Even Alerius took an interest in what Sean was doing and finally pulled Sean, Bruce, and Dar to his mountain. "This is the list of the names of those you chose as priestesses and the paladin candidates." He tapped a bundle of leather pages on a stone table. "This is a registry I have kept for all time. It is about the families that make up the tribes. Like the totems, I named them based on the totems. The candidates - they all come from just two tribes: Warg and Horse."

Dar was a member of Horse. "What does it mean?"

Alerius drummed his fingers in a very human mannerism. "Right now, nothing. Though a very long time ago, I allowed foreigners to join the tribes. It is not recorded or known to the people but every once in a while, I did this. I always brought them into other tribes than Horse or Warg. I saved those two tribes for heroes, the mighty, and anyone demonstrating exceptional skill in anything. Over time, Warg and Horse have become taller, stronger, healthier, and more intelligent. That is the only thing Warg and Horse have in common. They always had the best of the best."

Sean ran his finger down the list of names. "Amazing. You have a millennial ancestry record. Is there a family link to certain professions?"

Alerius shrugged. "Not that I have ever been able to tell. As your nation and others developed magi, knights, and assassins, I resigned myself for a time to dreaming of a mighty nation of warriors. And Time for my kind is very long indeed."

"My lord," Sean said after a moment. "There is something we must speak of. I do not think you will like it. But, I am compelled to speak it to you."

Alerius looked at him suddenly all dragon again. "I assure you Paladin Sean. You are in no position to know me well enough to know what I do and do not like."

"Very well. Your people, these people. They are dangerously close to worshipping Dar Tania as an intercessory. The legends, the religion, the stories of this people all lend themselves to what is called a 'cult of personality' in Taysor. It is a form of heresy. It corrupts pure worship of the divine to reliance on a person. To realize your vision, to truly worship the Goddess – or any god for that matter – this type of behavior thins conviction, and is too easily shaken should the person ever fail."

Alerius remained staring at him as he spoke. Dar finally asked, "So, some of them worship me instead of the Goddess?"

"I would say that they do not know who or how to worship. For all your history they have worshipped Alerius. Now there is a priestess able to heal and do things they dared not even imagine, even as we suddenly speak of a female Goddess. They have already started to convince themselves that you Dar are the Goddess."

Alerius hissed. "I see. How would they know that the Goddess' presence would destroy them in their current state? I see. We need to bind their faith faster than the Temple's construction will."

Sean spoke again, "My lord, you would have more priestess and paladin candidates if this heresy did not exist. Dare I say – Dar would have happened sooner if they worshipped the Goddess rather than you. Great King."

If Alerius seemed upset by his words, he gave no physical sign of it though the temperature around them had increased steadily word by word. At last he spat out a question, "You have some ideas?"

Sean nodded but wisely stayed quiet until Alerius calmed down.

Chapter 14 – For Consecration

All of them had been summoned to Alerius' throne chamber again. Syliri met them there draped in her robes and deep cowl. A note to them laid across a map explained that Alerius had marked the location of any number of dangerous monster lairs. Dar read the note translating the draconian. "Sean, you had this idea of a quest. Except for hunting for food, I have never taken a creature's life."

Bruce pointed to a symbol, "What is this close one?" Something about this strange lady called to him and he edged closer to her.

Syliri pointed touching his finger and with a smile in her voice said, "That is a displacer beast. There is a note that says it uses magic to appear slightly away from where it really is. There's another note that it is as strong as 8 heroes."

They pointed out a few others: pack of blink dogs, band of thieves, possible vampire and necromancer, griffins, stone sharks, and wyverns. These were the ones within several days march of Morbatten.

Sean looked at the map relishing its detail. "It's nice to have a map. In Taysor we usually get panicked reports through the militia and then the rangers are sent to investigate. Only sometimes do we have maps." He chuckled. "I've fought many of these. I like the idea of taking out the wyverns. It'd have some symbolic imagery as well. The blink dogs not so much. They can be trained and domesticated. Even if not, they are benign to peaceful people. Notice how there are no monsters in their area?"

They began talking with Sean and Bruce explaining what they knew about the various monsters. Syliri said, "The dragons saved these as tests for the people. Alerius felt these had a sense of destiny about them. My opinion, if you want it, is warm up on the thieves and then capture the vampire. The dragon king does so love to toy with the undead. It also falls in line with Sean's recommendation that the people see Dar fight using Tiamat's power. In short, and to your point, we need more priestesses and paladins to talk about Tiamat than just Dar and the dragon. This is perfect for that," she said tapping the thieves.

Dar introduced Syliri to the group, and then explained her nature. Both Sean and Bruce could not believe that a medusa could speak so beautifully. When she withdrew her hood, both men stared speechless and she blushed.

Bruce walked forward and kissed her hand. "I never imagined, nor will ever again consider medusae to be monsters."

She giggled, "Then you are a fool ranger. With Alerius' help, I have remained elevated and held my eldar state. Many of my sisters went mad when Time began charting their deaths. Or, they pledged themselves to the abyss. You are not repulsed by the snakes?"

Bruce stroked one not flinching as the snakes independently threatened to bite him. At his touch, she shuddered and her blush deepened. "As a ranger, I chose snakes as a natural language. I am fascinated by them." He turned to look at Sean. "I agree with Syliri. A warm up quest followed by the real one. A vampire as an evil foe is well-suited to our alignments and training. Though capture is not something we have ever done. That'll be new."

Sean agreed and created an excuse for Bruce and Syliri to be alone. It gave him a chance to talk with Dar and they sat on the ledge overlooking the valley. Dar began pointing and saying things like, "A great road shall run from there to there and be wide enough for 6 wagons to move on abreast! There will a fountain of dragons!"

The next day was the paladin test Sean had been preparing for. At dawn, he spoke to the hundreds gathered. "We have prepared an obstacle course. There are stations along the way where you will have to accomplish some task. This is a race. I cannot train all of you. The first twenty will continue as paladins. The next one hundred will wait two years before being trained by those twenty. If you are waiting, you will hasten your weapons training and combat skills. The last group will be designated as knights with a sole focus on combat training. In other words, you will not continue as paladins."

Bruce spoke next, "You heard the Captain, and it's a race. There is a flag for the first 120 atop Dragon Mountain, on the summit. Climbing the mountain, you will swim the lake by Soldier's Hill. Your flag has a scripture written on it in draconian. You must be able to read it to the priestesses at the top of Temple Hill. Lastly, you will face off in hand to hand combat here with any available warrior wearing a red headband. That's it."

A few of them indicated they had questions, but Sean pointed to the top of Dragon Mount and said, "Go!"

A few began walking, and then broke into a run. All at once, the entire group broke into a sprint. "Fools," Bruce laughed. "They'll be exhausted before they even make it to the base."

"You might be surprised. Running is a core skill we teach children. We even have a song for it – the Running Prayer."

"A prayer song?"

She began to sing it occasionally adding, "We have many songs. Stalking animals. Finding the north star. Making a fire. Preparing animal meat for food. Identifying animal foot marks. Knowing plants. Proper behavior when falling in love. Grieving the loss of a loved one. If Alerius thought it useful to survival, it became a way of life for us and songs to help children remember."

The priestess candidates identified earlier arrived and they began to prepare the field with wooden training staves, swords, and shields. Dar began singing a song and gradually, the ladies all joined in. Even Sean and Bruce tried though the draconian words made the ladies around them laugh. Food and drinks were placed around the perimeter and then the chieftains began to arrive. Most approached Dar and nodded their heads while touching their hearts with their right fist. One though walked straight up to Sean and without warning, struck his face.

Sean recoiled back as blood exploded from his nose and mouth. The chieftain said something that sounded insulting and then indicated Sean should draw his sword. Sean did not and instead called back, "Why? Why do you do this?"

The chief drew his sword in a slashing arc that would have cut Sean's outstretched hand. Just as the blade would cut, Dar caught the edge with her fingers. Her movement, just a blink of an eye, and then she stood resolute and unbleeding as the chief tried to pull back. His eyes wide and full of questions along with his pride, held him there.

Dar spoke and her voice rumbled like a dragon's as she said, "We are not at war with all of Taysor. By now, Alaura and Ynt'taris have declared it and brought Roland's kingdom to its knees. Your revenge is not with this one. Ever. Save it for winter. You will have as much blood as Roland sends us then."

Sean saw the rage dim though the chieftain still held his gaze and spat out, "You are lucky that a woman saves you!"

It seemed an innocent enough thing to say but suddenly, Dar ripped the sword out of his hand and spin-kicked the chieftain back. Caught off guard, he landed on his back. Twirling the sword around and catching the hilt she pointed it at him and said, very loudly, "Never forget *male* that the Goddess created all of us equal but that she has chosen a woman to lead you. I will not tolerate any consideration of women as being less than a male."

He sat up and bowed, "I hear and obey, but tell me - why? Why must we follow vendetta based on this foreigner's rules?"

"Isn't it obvious? Because I command it in Tiamat's name. The dragons chose females to hold their divine will. Not you. Not men. Now go. You are dismissed from this exercise. Go prepare your tribe for the Winter War."

Hours later, a puff of white cloud dotted the top of Dragon Mount. The first paladin candidate had made it to the top. Seeing it, Bruce marveled at the speed. "You may have ranger candidates in that group too."

Sean watched amazed as well and then added, "You can test the slower group. We need paladins first."

As the sun began to set, the first runner became visible. One of the priestesses noted it a girl from the Warg Tribe. Behind her, a handful of others quickly became visible. Of the first group, most came from the Warg tribe then Horse. Others noted it too and commented that it made sense the strongest tribe would quickly defeat a foreigner's obstacle course. Entering the field, they immediately, without rest, engaged in sparring combat with the chiefs.

Sean walked through the growing number of arrivals, watching their combat skill and making notes to a priestess trainee walking with him. Bruce also walked the group, watching and observing. Around midnight, they received word that there would be no more runners. While all had made the summit, it seems the slower members had counted the flags and seen they would not be considered. Set on completing the race, they all arrived the next morning.

Combat though lasted throughout the night. At some point, exhausted and tired, their opponent would throw or disarm them, or they suffered blunt damage that made it so they had to stop. To each of these, Sean would approach, order them to take a five minute rest, and then re-engage. This cycle repeated and repeated. As sunshine crested the eastern ranges, just five remained. And then there was only one.

"Dar," Sean called out. "We are done. All of you, return to your people and rest. Prepare yourselves for your first quest."

To the twenty who lasted the longest, Sean smiled and said, "Congratulations! You will be the first though you have all shown us something we had not considered. Do any of you enjoy the wilderness – the magic of nature?" To the first one who had made it through all the tests Sean asked, "Tell me, your name and tribe?"

The young man, he could not have been older than sixteen, stood proud and said, "I am Shak d'Rath of the Warg Tribe Captain Sean. I will be the first paladin!"

Chapter 15 – Den of Thieves

Captain Sean stood by his heavy charger. Gilded plate mail gleamed in the early morning's sunlight. Overhead, his pinion snapped and danced, its many brightly colored streams radiating from the sun seamed magical in the wind's movement. Dar stared at him until one of the two new priestesses elbowed her and they giggled. He looked powerful, dashing, handsome, and ready for war while at the same time looking clean and polished. In contrast, Bruce stood by Syliri. His ranger garb already trying to blend in to the forest behind him. He and Syliri held hands and Dar overheard him say how glad he was she had decided to come along. It made her feel a bit lonely. Too much of her life since becoming a priestess had been away from the people.

As the eight paladins arrived, Dar felt them starring at the Captain. A girl barely older than fourteen, a mother of two and a renowned warrior in her tribe, and then six men had made it to the final eight of Sean's paladin trials. They looked excited and ready if a bit unsure of themselves. Sean ordered them to form a line and then walked down the line asking a few questions about the leather armor they used. Some tribes had figured out how to repurpose armor captured from their skirmishes. Though worked into the leather, Sean's armor made it seem drab and ineffective. One area where Morbatten did not suffer though was in the quality of its weaponry. Though not as designed and ornate as Sean and Bruce's, their swords gleamed sharp and deadly.

Dar spoke to them, introducing their roles and informing them about the mission. "This group of thieves, though out of the people's lands, could be a threat. We are going to find them. Eliminate them. If we do well, we will then face a deadly enemy from beyond death. Consider the thieves a training exercise, for you all to get to know each other."

One of the new paladins asked if she would be their leader. Before she could answer, Sean did. "The goddess leads, speaking to Dar Tania. She is our leader but where combat is concerned, I am your commander. Let's move out."

Bruce immediately vanished into the forest. Within Morbatten, the people came out and cheered their departure. Against her vision of a vast empire, the sudden end to the small valley felt depressing. She moved up to speak with Sean. Soon, the road and then the miles of trails rolled by and they made excellent time once Sean and Bruce realized they could move much faster than Taysor groups did.

They set up camp with Dar and the priestesses retreating to prayer. If the map showed distance accurately, they would reach the thieves' location in three days' time. Still flushed with excitement, the camp did not sleep early or well. With Bruce and Syliri sitting back on a log and talking, Sean began speaking about discipline and shared stories from Taysor that highlighted the life, vows, and expectations of a paladin. At one point, after a story of forbidden love, one of the new paladins asked why they could not love.

"It has always been that way," he shrugged. "Over time, there have been doctrines, teachings, and reasons for it put forth but the original reason is that the first paladins of Pha Rann were all chaste." In response to the inevitable 'what if' question, he continued, "If I did, I would be breaking my vows to abstain. I would lose my standing as a paladin. I would have to atone."

"That's stupid," Dar interjected from her discussion. Clearly, she had tuned into their conversation. "I will ensure that paladins here are not bound by such bad rules." Even as she said it though, something felt off. The others felt it too and she quickly added, "If the Goddess is okay with it."

Sean met her gaze and added, "Morbatten is full of fighters. You are a nation of fighters that have skills above that of most fighters from my land. But, to go from that to being something specialized – whether a paladin like me, a ranger like Bruce, a priest like Jeffreys, or I would add a sorcerer like the dragon king – sacrifices are made. These sacrifices can be unconscious ones where you do not even realize it. But at some point, conscious sacrifices are made. I chose to be this and made vows of poverty, chastity, and servitude to the Bright God Pha Rann. Perhaps the Goddess will not require the same sacrifices. I cannot know."

At some point, watchmen took up the watch and the others slept. Time on the trail was fast as everyone seemed to be racing to the thieves. That second night, Sean put out a question about tactics. "Do the paladins need a song to focus them spiritually? You are all too full of combat lust. You'll never hear your Goddess like this. As holy warriors of your Goddess, you have to be able to hear your god, even in combat, even when wounded or taking life. I want you all to be silent. Kneel. Close your eyes. Focus on what your Goddess wants you to do. Dar, as they do this, I want you to bless them."

At his orders, the camp went silent immediately. Dar looked questioningly at him but then began to pray in her soft singing voice. "I feel her power," she said after a few moments. One by one, she lightly touched the foreheads. At her touch, some got cold chills along their skin while others felt a rush of air around them. Sounds from the fire, the forest, their surrounding comrades, all amplified and each felt a curious thing.

Finally one said, "The Goddess does not like the Captain very much."

Sean chuckled. "Good, you're in touch. Good. And no, she does not. There is enmity from your Goddess to mine. I can only imagine the ironic sense of my being here. There are knights in my nation that would quest, would do anything for a chance to challenge your goddess in mortal combat. However, for my part, I am not such a one. I see a balance amongst the gods and a great purpose here that will serve the world."

Another said, "This is funny. I feel as if the Goddess is amused at the sacrifices your god requires you to make. Why?"

Sean stirred the fire listening to Dar as she sang and moved through the group. "Every deity rules over something. That *something* is what gives them power. It is their dominion. Any other power touching or interacting with that dominion, adds to that dominion's power. As such, you have very powerful dominions like Creation, Death, Good, and Evil. You also have powerful but narrow dominions like Justice, or Vengeance though these dominions are not as powerful compared to say Creation. Right now, Dar is *creating* a new experience for each of you. In Morbatten, a new religion is being *created*. When we made the fire, we *created* fire. Our everyday actions add to the dominion of Creation. Our acts of creation do nothing for Justice, at this time. As such, the dominion of Justice is generally less powerful than Creation. However, in a moment of righteous fury, should you decide to choose Justice over revenge, should you choose Justice when everything in and around you screams for something else, in that moment, the dominion of Justice is supremely powerful. Do you understand?"

Heads nodded until Dar asked, "Your sun god claims Creation?"

Sean poked the fire with a long stick and stirred the embers. "Pha Rann is the Creator. His dominion is therefore every and anything ever created and yet to be created. Moreover, destruction lends itself to the creation of new possibilities. Extending this, when evil and vile monsters give birth to offspring, this too is an act of creation. This is all Pha Rann's dominion. His power is there whether the monsters realize it or not. That same power that births demons births heroes."

Dar smiled and said, "Hear me now children of the dragons. The Goddess claims this world as the created work of dragons and us as Her own. This is where we disagree with Captain Sean."

He just smiled and continued to stir the embers. "When I serve the Pha Rann's purposes, I add to his dominion not through some instinctual act of creation but by conscious choice and faith. This increases Pha Rann's dominion into my actions whether they are Creation or not. By sacrificing parts of myself to that dominion, I obtain divine favor. It allows me to heal quickly, grants immunity to poison and disease, and allows me to detect the evil intent of those around me. Since arriving here, I have felt almost no evil intent, even from the dragons. I feel intent that is counter to Pha Rann's purposes, but it is not evil. Not yet. The question you should consider is what sacrifices might your Goddess require of you?"

One of the candidates said, "It doesn't matter. Whatever she requires, whatever the dragons require, we will do." It seemed so cavalier and naïve, but when the others cheered it with great seriousness, Sean realized how thoroughly indoctrinated this entire people had become. The conversation continued until they took rest.

The party awoke to Bruce galloping into camp just before sunrise. "I've got them!" he exclaimed. "The thieves, I've found their location! It's about a three hour march from here."

By the time he finished saying this, the Tanians had armed and stood at the ready. "Excellent," Sean said observing their reactions, even after hard marching on the road. "Let's make ready."

While they broke camp, Bruce explained how a box canyon rose between two rocky hills. A cave therein located them with two rotating guards on lookout, one just in the cave and one from up on the box canyon. "The rocks are loose. I'd imagine they'd hear and see anyone approaching. I also found a chimney to vent smoke and heat farther back on the southern side of the canyon's top."

With camp cleared and everyone ready, they moved off at a run. Dar Tania and Sean on their horses talked strategy. "This is simple but with the paladins, I want a decisive victory. The chimney makes it too easy. We block that, eventually, they'll all come out of the cave or send a few to investigate. My tribe would kill or capture them and move in for the kill. It'd be done and over."

Sean replied to her, "Very wise and agreed. Two things though. There might be other chimneys. And we don't know yet if they truly are thieves." Seeing her frown, he quickly added, "The dragon king did not indicate when he made the notes or what exactly he felt by labeling them thieves. Isn't it safe to say that our understanding of what a thief is may differ from a dragon's?"

Dar considered it. "His map indicated only threats that the patriarchs were watching. To label them thieves, he must have seen them stealing or acting like thieves. Though I see your point. We don't really have thieves in Morbatten. The tribes move around a lot. Sometimes people take things but when it is known and done openly, we don't consider it stealing. Draconian for thief actually is closer to someone who is *quick*. It's most often a compliment. Your use of the word though, for us, would be a criminal."

Sean listened to her and mulled over the possibilities. "Maybe the dragon king noted this to mean a fast enemy?" He shrugged.

Chapter 16 – Battle of the Thieves

Nothing had gone right. Blocking the chimney had failed to drawn anyone out. Though they had not alerted the guards, they had tried and failed to get close enough to capture and question the overwatch. Each time, the loose rocks betrayed them far away enough that they retreated. Sean watched, offering no assistance other than words of encouragement.

Finally, Dar asked why not just attack. Frustrated and growing tired, the rest of the group agreed. Sean nodded and said, "Okay, good. You have a new plan. Remember though, you're holy knights. Do you know your enemy? Are they actually your enemy? Is this what your Goddess wants you to do?"

Confused faces turned to each other. Though Dar had discussed this with Sean, no one else had. A voice muttered, "If I don't do something I'm going to scream."

Teasing laughter tittered through the group before Dar said, "Are you suggesting a different way?"

Sean shook his head, "No, no. I'm here to help. I do not want the first Tanian adventure to be one about Taysor. It has to be Morbatten, for Morbatten, by Morbatten."

Everyone turned to look at Dar. She took a deep breath, "We'll be on guard and approach the cave. If they attack, we'll know they are enemies."

Dar and Sean guided their horses towards the cave mouth. In front of them, their knights walked trying to mask their combat interest with faces forced to look tired and road weary. Somewhere, Bruce shadowed their movements. Under leather and animal hide cloaks and travel robes, the Tanians gripped their weapons and prayed for a chance to prove themselves to the Goddess, but mostly to the Priestess Dar.

When an arrow struck the ground paces ahead of them, they stopped and Dar called out asking for a conversation and assistance. Beside her, Sean whispered, "This is it. Will they talk or fight?"

They saw it coming from miles away. The arrows launched, the stones thrown, and the road behind them blocked by logged pushed down by what appeared to be ogres. Only a few arrows came close and only one close enough to matter. One of the paladins caught it and dropped it to the ground. Black ichor dried on the arrowhead suggested poison.

The afternoon wind stirred the trees and plants dotting the box canyon a few moments before ogres crouching behind boulders, and the ones behind them, roared their charge. Dar called out, "I count seven of the beasts. Take their heads!"

The Tanians broke into a charge moving forward. The two ogres behind blinked in confusion as the only capable looking one, Caption Sean was suddenly joined by an oddly-armored human who came out of nowhere.

The ogres, taking this group for easy prey, smashed into the Tanian knights and roared out their victory cries before the pain of deep and piercing sword cuts registered. One ogre speared through its chest by two Tanian blades looked up in confusion to see Dar. He heard her sing, "Dragonfire take you," before its pain changed to searing pain as its body ignited.

Like a rallying cry, the other priestesses began copying Dar, and though had lesser effect, their targeted enemies began to smolder and burn. Taking heart from this, the new paladins stopped dodging attacks and waiting for orders from Sean or Dar and engaged fully their enemy.

One of the paladins found himself confronted by a wounded ogre backed up by a shoddy looking human. The ogre hurled a head sized rock at him. Though he dodged to the side, an arrow fired by the human pierced the leather hides and metal scale armor just enough to slow him down. The ogre laughed thinking him now an easy target. Normally, the warrior would shrug off the pain and berserk his enemy. *Victory at any cost*, a saying popular amongst the tribes. This time though, he felt something stir in the back of his mind and heart. A whispered female voice urged him to listen. He did. As the ogre came in to smash him with a club, the paladin stood on guard. As the ogre raised his club, he stepped into the ogre's personal space. The Tanian blade skewered the beast through its worn armor and stopped its heart even as a misfired arrow thudded into the ogre's back shoulder.

As if applause now, the knight heard the feminine voice cry out in pleasure and delight and pride as if you to tell him he had done well. Never before had he felt this way. This must be the Goddess, he thought as he turned his focus from impressing the others to serving Tiamat. At the Goddess' elation singing in his heart, he forgot about his wound – the arrow still sticking through his armor. The shoddy human attempted to reload and fire but seeing the serene unafraid countenance of this warrior step aside from the collapsing ogre's hulk, he fumbled the nock, and met his death by decapitation. Again, that chorus of elation… and then another whisper in his heart, urged him to step aside and cut backwards. Blood spraying from the just slain archer sprayed back in a circle as his blade circled back and met another thief intent on backstabbing him.

Silence everywhere. The new paladin saw everything moving as if in slow motion. Only the Taysorian fighters and Dar moved in normal speed and he heard a chorus of praise, a choir song of fire, blood, and death around Dar Tania. Streams of light and energy moved around the field of war in that canyon. Motes of light and energy brushed off his enemies and he saw those he had killed, their bodies dark grey, bleeding light and energy into nothingness. Suddenly, his awareness opened and shifted. He stood now in that canyon but a current of energy flowed through it and him. He marveled and almost fell to worship this strange power, except that Captain Sean caught his gaze. Through the vasty silence of this pause in combat, Sean said, "Seize this. Hold it. Channel it to your sword and praise your Goddess!" Sean imitated the knight dipping his sword into the current of energy.

When the new paladin did, his sword erupted in dark red, almost purple flames. The fire did not burn or even warm him, but plants and the bodies of his slain enemies began to smoke in its heat and then they ignited. He became aware of Dar. She called to him, "May the Goddess guide you Shak D'Rath! Now fight!" He marveled at her never before realizing how awesomely beautiful she had become. He looked around to see if others noticed the slow motion effect, but his fellow initiates were all caught mid-action, barely moving.

A fellow knight near him felt the heat of Shak's sword ignite and in a blink, Shak cut the arm clean off the ogre about to end him. The heat of the sword cauterized the wound instantly and threw the beast into shock. Streams of movement, like action echoed in mere instants, tore Shak from that enemy to another and then another. And then it was over.

Though wounded, none of their party had died. The wounded quickly recovered under the healing prayers of the priestesses. Shak's blade flickered seeking more enemies and he looked around as everyone stared at him. "Don't be alarmed. This will become commonplace to each of you. Shak," as Captain Sean spoke he ignited his own sword. It glowed like the noon day sun. "Well done. You listened to your Goddess and she blessed you. Your sword, actually any sword is now your avenger. This tool is gifted to paladins to use at their discretion, but never against your Goddess' will. It is not to be trifled with. You must treat it as sacred. Do you understand?"

Shak nodded. "How do I make it stop?" He trembled and then began to shake violently. Bruce caught him before he collapsed bringing him water.

Dar spoke now to Shak, and the others. "Shak, you were the first to complete the tests in Morbatten. Here in the Vale of First Battle you are the first to breach the river of time and ignite your sword. Well done! I would speak to you now about the river.

"For the eldar, this is how the dragon emperor and his brothers call those before time, there was no time. This world, our world progresses from night to day. Fire burns and leaves ashes. Time takes us through these moments, but it was not like this for the eldar. They call the flow of time different things but the dragon emperor calls it 'the river'. The river flows from the moment of our creation to the moment of our deaths. The emperor would tell you the river is death and disease. But it is also power. Shak, you stepped out of the river and used that power to destroy your enemies. Quench your blade in the river and enter back into it."

At her command, Shak attempted to stand but his shaking returned and he fell unconscious. Immediately his sword's fire went out. Bruce laid him gently down and said, "Accessing the river is hard. Both to do and then to stay out of its flow for even a moment. The first time especially. Your force of will holds you there. It gets easier with familiarity but you can only stay so long as your will can hold you there. Think of it as trying to fight two enemies with two different weapons – like a sword and a cudgel, each on either side of you. Though not impossible, eventually even someone trained to do this will fall. The difference of what you're familiar with and having to divide your attention, well, it is very hard. Not everyone can do it."

A warrior asked, "If we cannot, will we not continue as paladins?"

Dar answered, "You will continue as paladins. Your worthiness and faith are what set you apart. The ability to access the river is different. And a rare gift. It's more akin to my becoming the first to fly with the dragon emperor. You will all become paladins except unless you are unable to sacrifice what is required of you."

They looked at Shak wondering what sacrifices he might be making even then.

Chapter 17 – Breaching the Den

They heard the mouth of the cave seal closed as boulders were rolled to block the entrance. Shak had started to recover but was not yet able to stand. Sean called for them to rest since they were not in any immediate danger. Later, Bruce returned and said the cave entrance had been blocked but archers waited behind the barricade to shoot at them through cracks.

More time passed before Tania called them together. "I have a plan," she stated simply. Listening to it, Shak and the others began to grin.

Each paladin initiate stood in front of a priestess. They formed two columns alternating like that. Sean and Tania followed Bruce's lead to the entrance being careful to avoid areas where they would be targeted by archers. This put them right to the side of the cave entrance. The others lined up with the priestesses against the canyon wall and each paladin stretching and getting ready. Silence was no issue. Each paladin and each priestess carried skins full of water.

Tania bowed her head and prayed to the Goddess. At her words, a pillar of fire rose up from the ground in front of the cave mouth. Sean snapped his visor down and gripped his sword as the flames danced and wove next to the barricade. Coaxed by Tania's prayer, the flames burst and roared reaching hundreds of feet into the sky even as the stone and ground nearby began to glow red and then white. The prayer went on and on as beads of sweat gathered and then fell down Tania's face and body. Every once in a while, an arrow would shoot blindly into the flames and cinder before striking anything.

Tania's voice, hoarse and barely a whisper now, urged the flames hotter, brighter, and stronger. With each insistence, they obeyed. At last, her final words spoke and for one brief moment, the fire roared like a dragon's breath against the rock wall and into the sky. As the divine heat vanished, the paladins rushed forward and threw their water skins and then the priestesses' skins against the barricade. An explosion of steam and hissing fury hid the sound of the priestesses blessing their chosen warriors with resistance to heat.

Shak and the others, as the blessings cooled their singed faces, rushed forward and began kicking and shoving the burning rocks back into the cave. As hastily erected the barricade had been, and blasted by magic and water, the rocks quickly fell until a hole large enough for a single fighter to pass opened. Into this opening, Sean dove expecting a volley of arrows.

Rolling to his knees and guarding himself with his shield, he saw that the archers had perished in the heat of the fire. Perhaps some had tried to flee, but the sword cuts through the throats of those facing away from the entrance showed what had happened to them. He whistled to signal the passage had been cleared. Not surprised to see Shak enter first, Sean pointed down the passage and said, "No doubt they chose to make their stand further down."

The two of them moved forward as the others entered with the priestesses. Sean ignited his sword for light until they at last came to an open room roughly carved into the rock. Water dripped into a small pool from one wall. The buckets and cookware near the water showed this to be their water source. A stench rose from a passage to the right. The left looked better traveled.

Sean grinned behind his helmet when Shak took the mission to heart and told the others, "This is OUR mission. The right passage suggests a monster but in this case, I feel we should send a stronger force to the other." He pointed to three and said, "You guard our flanks. Priestesses in the middle. The rest on me."

Sean's grin split into a bright smile when he saw the others automatically follow Shak's orders. Even the priestesses obeyed and Sean watched Tania, exhausted as she was, move into the center. Sean signaled this to Bruce who grinned at him.

Moving forward, a clatter of poorly aimed arrows showered down around them. Shak caught one in his thigh, but it barely pierced his armor. About half the group carried shields and Shak moved this group forward. The tunnel lit so the archers could see, allowed Shak to see.

Another barricade about waist high made of furniture and wood blocked them about thirty feet ahead. Archers popped up from this and shot at them from time to time. Realizing that delaying made them easier targets, Shak commanded the soldiers to throw their daggers and charge. The archers ducked for cover and though not a single dagger struck a target, the knights easily leapt the barricade and found what was left of the thieves. Three archers, one with horrible burn wounds, and an ogre with blistered skin immediately turned to attack them. While the ogre put up some resistance, they were no match for this group. Before the ogre fell, one of the archers died. With the ogre being cut down, the last two humans dropped their weapons and surrendered.

Just in time for Sean to walk in and see Shak kneel before Tania. Her voice wounded from her prayers, she mustered the strength to congratulate them. "Well done! Such fury to do the Goddess proud. Your fury is beautiful," she said to Shak. She touched his forehead and he rose clearly pleased.

The others smiled and again, Sean was impressed with their combat savvy when Shak, ordered the priestesses to secure the prisoners and to take the other passage. This time, their preparation and combat lust could not be satisfied. No barricade greeted them. No archers sat in wait. Instead, they found a dismal room of children, no – not children, halflings. All bore the signs of having been beaten and a few were long dead. All were starving and had the look of those awaiting death in their eyes. They barely moved when Shak and the others burst into their midst.

Sean pulled Tania back and asked her, "Has the dragon emperor ever spoken of halflings to you?" She shook her head no and was about to ask if they were children or monsters or something else but Sean interrupted her. "You have a chance make a powerful alliance here. Trust me. We must save them. They are a good folk."

Tania nodded and called to Shak, "We have rescued these *halflings*. Organize the group and help get them outside and cleaned up. Have the priestesses attend to those not yet too wounded to save. I'll see what I can for the others."

They found forty-five halflings in that hellhole. The oldest, now permanently blinded, explained only after he touched and recognized Sean's holy symbol of the Sun God. "One hundred of us left to seek a new colony, to settle down and build our lives anew after a flood destroyed our homes. I don't know how long it has been. The ogres wiped out those of us who could fight and captured the rest of us. They used our possessions to attract some humans." He winced rubbing his hands together. "The ogres were saving and eating us, like food. Who does that? My wife – " he began to sob.

The warriors stood back not knowing what to make of these child-like short adults. Similar stories began to come out of pain, loss of loved ones, torture, and other crimes too horrible to tell that brought them to tears. The stoic Tanians found these halflings stirred their emotions and made them want to help. Tania sat down by the elder and said, "You're safe now. I promise. We have destroyed all of them except a few of the humans. Here is one if you would like his life as revenge." At her gesture, the priestesses kicked the man to the ground.

The elder looked up and though anger filled his eyes and heart to the point Tania felt him tremble, the halfling said, "No revenge could satisfy our losses and suffering. To take revenge in this manner would belittle the cost of what we have lost."

"Very well. I have no use for this thing." She gave the order to kill the archer, but the elder interrupted her.

"Please, do not. Enough have died."

"Excuse me," Tania said. "You don't understand. This human participated in your loss and fought against my people. He is evil and must die." Again, she went to signal execution but the elder caught her hand.

"Great lady who saved us. My apologies for speaking so abruptly when you are our savior but it is you who do not understand. If all we do is repay evil with evil, then evil wins. At some point, we must rebalance the scales. It may very well be that this man deserves death, but I ask you. No I beg you, please do not do this. Let him go."

The Tanians began laughing at how ludicrous it would to let this captured enemy just leave. Instead she called out, "Syliri, will you bring the emperor's justice to these two so that they do not die?"

From the wall, out of the stone, Syliri appeared. The halfling elder recoiled back from her presence feeling something monstrous even as the other few halflings with him said, "Medusa! Cover your eyes!"

Syliri took the human thief's in her hands and said, "Look at me human." He did not but a few snake bites later, he did. Looking into her eyes, a beatific expression of calm washed over his fear and concern and then his body turned to stone.

The halflings whimpered. "Who are you that monsters serve you?"

"I am Dar Tania, priestess of Tiamat of the empire of Morbatten." She was about to go on and tell him more but in that moment, something stirred in her. A vision opened in her mind. South and east of the temple, long lay hilly grasslands that rose up onto a wet and verdant plateau. Their people had long used it only as a crossroads, but in her vision, she saw lush farmlands and water-powered mills sustaining and feeding her armies. Her body jerked to the point she almost fell except that Sean caught her

"What is your name?" she asked of the halfling.

The elder said, "My wife's name was Katie Riverwheel. Mine is Summer."

"Summer Riverwheel. My goddess has shown me that you will survive this dark chapter in your settlement journey. If you will come with us, I will lead you to a land of water and fertile grounds."

Summer's eye sockets brightened with a short spark of hope and then dimmed when he asked, "And the price for this paradise?"

"You will become part of Morbatten and serve the dragons, like Captain Sean here. Your gods and your political will shall remain your own."

"But we will be your slaves – "

"No, you will be our brothers and sisters. In time, your children will join into our vision and a few will serve in the mightiest ranks of Morbatten. Until then, we will buy and trade for the crops you will produce and the foods you will secure." Tania laughed. "We thrive in combat, but lack the patience to farm. Had the Goddess not shown me this, I'd have never guessed at these things."

A few of the others limped over to Summer asking if this could be true. With tears in his eyes, he wept and held them and looked up at Tania. "I want to believe priestess, I do. But you do not serve the Sun God like this one here. We do. I fear betrayal."

The Tanians bristled at this comment and leapt to Tania's defense but she waved them back sternly with rebuke in her eyes. "You have suffered much Summer. You and your people deserve hope. If the Goddess wills it, I shall show the vision."

Tania took Summer's knotted and broken hands in her own, healing and warmth radiating in his bones. Caught up in healing prayer, Summer's vision jumped to the River and he saw himself and Tania standing in a swiftly flowing current of death. However, an eddy in that current caught his attention and as he looked more closely at it, it filled his view with the vision Tania had seen. Suddenly, he stood in a meadow of wheat and corn to the side of a squash and melon patch. Butterflies danced in the late summer air, warm on his face. Blocky Tanians like his rescuers called out for crop forecasts and asked when they could buy another cart of summer vegetables. High overhead, a dragon caught the breeze but instead of filling him with dread, in the vision at least the dragon made him feel known and treasured.

Behind the cart, a marketplace of laughing children chased each other. He saw these dark-haired and gruff people walking amidst his offspring peaceably and saw several elves and dwarves as well. Then the vision ended and he found himself back in the canyon. "It's true. It's all true," he said. More tears and then the halflings all were crying and hugging each other. Those embraces caught up the Tanians as well who awkwardly and stiffly returned the hugs.

When the priestesses began walking through and tending to wounds, the halflings broke out in song as Summer described his vision. "What will we name this paradise?" one of the survivors called out.

Tania smiled down at River. "You shall call it Home."

Chapter 18 – So It Begins

The Halfling nation, proudly called Home, was the first. The story of Shak the Wrathful, first legendary hero of Morbatten and the tongue of flames that lashed the thieves was handwritten by Alerius into the Book of Genesis. The people witnessed the dragon emperor write Tania's words atop the hill of three stone columns.

Other stories followed in fast order as Shak formed his own group of heroes and warriors flocked to the paladins for adventure. The borders of Morbatten enlarged and the children of the dragons, their stories, and their culture began in earnest. That is not to say it was easy. Birthing a nation is never easy. But with hope, a vision, a beautiful leader, and under the watchful eye of eternal dragons, it is easier.

Bruce and Syliri took it on themselves to wander the land and identify other risks that perhaps a dragon would not care about but a mortal would. Sean remained at Tania's side until one day, she demanded that he marry her. Their agreement that their children would receive teachings about both gods and when teens could choose their own path set a tone of religious tolerance that the tribes had never had. Though Sean and the halflings' belief and worship of the Sun God Pha Rann never really resonated with the Tanians, a healthy respect grew because Shak of Fury deferred and gave respect to Sean.

One summer day at sunset, the trinity of dragons sat on the stone columns. They watched the small spark of lights come alive as night fell and the blue dragon patriarch said, "You have exceeded even your expectations brother Alerius."

Ynt'taris also noted, "Each day Tanians arrive with fragments of the Queen's vision. You have a priestess, a hero paladin, an alliance of sorts, and halflings. What is next?"

Alerius craned his head to the north star. "This forge must turn a few cycles before it shall be broken. Brothers, undead will raid and destroy my children almost to the brink. A darkness rises against us. You have seen this."

The white and blue nodded but Spark answered first, "The darkness that is the necromancer will come to take the hellhound back."

"And we will be ready. Though it costs us a nation, my children will be strong enough to endure and the reward will be beyond imagining."

Ynt'taris grinned. "I cannot see how it will be any other way. Bloodstones."

"Eldar magic in this fallen world," Spark crooned. "It will be glorious."

"At a price that may be too high but, yes. Brothers we must be ready. My children must be ready. Ynt'taris, the priestesses must step far enough in time that Tania and her acolytes are here when the Necromancer comes. Spark, all must have passion beyond pain if they are to survive. I see a valley ringed by fortresses, drenched in blood. We must take our battle with the Necromancer from this valley, our treasure horde, to the mountain."

"Tania will soon give birth to a daughter," Ynt'taris said. "After, I will begin instructing her in the ways of Time and how to slow it."

"Within a generation, I will enact Consecration amongst your children and that will bind them to the Mother so that passion beyond pain is theirs," Spark promised.

Alerius listened and after a pause spoke, "Within a generation, my sons shall arrive with the kerchki veiled. They shall become the backbone of my children. In their hearts we shall kindle an eternal fire that will only grow brighter against the darkness that comes. For those that survive, they will become a second genesis."

"Mother grants you her fire giants?" Ynt'taris asked.

"She does brother. Efforts to win allegiance of the other giants have failed though. I share your sadness."

Ynt'taris deflated at the emperor's words but with cold steel and intent, the white dragon broke the pregnant silence. "Alaura's children shall take their place. I will teach her to slay the frost giants, and break them."

The other two looked askance at the white who finally explained. "Alaura has seen wickedness in her own faith. She will come to us of her own will soon. A pairing between her and any member of the Warg tribe will birth a new tribe of winter wolves, and they shall be mine."

"Very well," Alerius agreed. "The Tribe of the Winter Wolf shall be joined to the Ancients and be our wall to the north against which Taysor shall learn to fear us. Your Winter War."

More lights twinkled into being below as the night drew on. "Fire Patriarch, I hope the bloodstones are worth it," Spark observed. "Your children already shine brighter than any treasure of the old worlds."

"The daughter to be born of Tania and Sean will shine the brightest, and bring us the Temple and my people's consecration to our mother," Alerius said. "I see that Bruce and Syliri will order rangers for us, without our asking. I see what will be and it is glorious. Even without the bloodstones. The cost still gives me pause."

Spark broke the long silence of the growing night. "Brother, the bloodstones are key. Though I do not envy the price. Many of your children will die."

Ynt'taris now spoke, "Prophecy whispers to me that a child born of the Warg tribe, named Bomoki, shall bring forth the ram into our valley of treasure."

"Yes. We will know but cannot act. For my children to become a spear head they must be forged in fire and blood first. Though potent, they lack refining. The prophecy hurts. Warg gives us many of our most precious children. That just one will bring this on us is appalling."

Ynt'taris craned his head to the north where the peaks of the Shield Mountains glimmered too far away for a human to see. "Soon, winter will be here. This dark prophecy will wait for the forge to turn a few more times great lord of fire."

Epilogue

A brief study of Morbatten's history is not required. It is common knowledge after all that Dar Tania served as high priestess, the first of many. She completed the Temple At Morbatten and the grand road to Alerius' palace. The halflings settled in what is now called Home. Morbatten became a bustling hub of activity, construction, and learning.

Captain Sean remained true to his paladin vows, even when Dar ordered him to marry her. Instead, he founded the paladin orders and led them, always at Dar's side. While waiting, and at Alerius' command, Dar took several husbands and bore children that considered Sean their foreign uncle. Later in life, when Sean had fought enough, he retired and free of all vows, asked Dar Tania to marry him. They had a daughter together.

Bruce and Syliri created a ranger core that sought out and mapped the borders of the nation, and brought back new monsters for Alerius' museum. Shak proved himself not just a genius paladin, but when the time came, instead of a horse, he quested and returned with a griffin. His children and those few with a similar gift created a new Tribe of the Griffin.

Alaura built a palace on the grand road at the base of Alerius' mountain and became an apprentice sage, recording stories told by Ynt'taris and the others where possible. For a time, Ynt'taris let go of his enmity to mortals and taught Alaura all he knew about frost and ice giants. Alaura became the ice patriarch's rider. When Alaura died, Ynt'taris never quite recovered. Her death pulled him too far down the flow of time, and he aged.

Bards came to learn those stories and soon the tales of Morbattania – now Tania for short and out of respect for Dar Tania herself – came to be known across the isles. The zealot knights of Taysor, called *Rolands* by Tania, came for Winter War each year. Sometimes it raged with wooden sticks and good manners. Other times, it spilled out of the mountains and became actual war.

This story sets the foundation for the Forsaken Isles. If you enjoyed this, please visit Dar Malcor's blog, the second paladin king of Tania at darmalcor.weebly.com Also, the adventures of the second king are available as Malcor's Story. An excerpt appears below. Bomoki's Gate continues the legend of Malcor, to be released in March 2017.

Excerpted from Malcor's Story...

King Rojo's whisper and a hand on Malcor's shoulder called him to stand. He rose and with surprise found himself at eye to eye level with the King's eyes. He almost did a double-take when he noticed flecks, many flecks of varying color embedded into those eyes, but not a hint of affection or mirth lay therein. "Your name is Malcor correct? Your words are true, but this is not what you feel. Turn and face your *R'Dar* – inflected as *slave master* – and tell him who you are. Impress me Malcor-who-dreams-of-being-a-paladin."

Just before turning to confront R'dar Tor, Malcor thought of the correct politically-wise thing to do. But, he saw Armageddon give him a warning glance, as if a dragon had facial expressions. He felt that fire in his heart again and knew.

The courtyard's silence felt stifling. R'dar Tor's expression, well known after years of servitude, seemed caught between deferred respect/fear of the King and disdain for Malcor. He could end all of this by declaring himself a smith, and returning to the forge. But, those days spent walking the hills and listening to wind in the grass and the knights' stories about town begged him to not be just a smith. If only... no, it was now or never. *This is my trial.*

"R'dar Tor, I have worked with you since my master adopted me." Malcor drew the long sword from the scabbard tied to his bag. His hands shook and he saw Tor snicker at it. But the rage in his soul threatened to break him to pieces. In the silent moment, its keen edge resonated shrill and clear. He heard a murmuring rise up from the crowd, especially the knights nearby, *See the apprentice's sword!*

"I have dreamed of being a knight, of serving the Empire, of fighting for the Queen. My destiny is not at the forge. It is out there, westwards." He pointed his sword tip at R'dar Tor's forehead. "I am not yours. I am free."

A vein on Tor's head pulsed in the growing twilight wreathed about by fire from lanterns, from the dragons themselves, and from the last rays of sunlight. Faster than Malcor thought possible, the R'Dar drew his rapier and drew a cut along Mal's cheek... or at least that is what should have happened. Instead, Mal slipped out of the River for just a moment where a thunderous and deadly female voice roared in his ears, "Kill him my son and you will be a knight!"

The command hurt his ears as he dove back into the River somehow stepping below the cut and spinning around the R'dar's body to the right. Crouched low at Tor's side, Mal saw the man wide open and then wide-eyed as he realized the youth had vanished and reappeared in the worst possible place for a counter or defense.

The R'dar tried to spin aside but as if hammering iron at the forge – *does the smith think about the pain of the metal as it cooks and melts or is struck by hammer blow upon hammer fell?* – Mal impaled his sword up through the R'dar's rib cage, spearing the man's heart and exiting just through the right shoulder. Blood dribbled from the man's lips as his head and face starred at the exited blade point. He seemed as if to say something and then, without another thought, Malcor twisted the blade as he yanked it out. "I am not yours," he screamed into the R'dar's dying face. The R'dar's corpse collapsed like a bag of meat.

And silence… in the courtyard… not a sound and then one of the dragons leaned forward and bit the man off the ground. A slight head twist and the R'dar vanished into a maw of teeth and fire. More moments passed, and the King spoke again breaking the silence.

"Not a very usual Coming of Age ceremony, but one we shall not forget. But for that fool of a merchant – what was his name? – we might have a king. But it has been revealed and the prophecy fulfilled! Dar Shara, let the Temple send word to the Merchant's Guild that," a scribe whispered to the King, "R'Dar Tor of Klenna is dead, slain in fair and witnessed combat before myself and all others. Make a note that the usual rules apply for belongings and deeded properties."

www.ingramcontent.com/pod-product-compliance
Lightning Source LLC
Chambersburg PA
CBHW070638130626
46555CB00006B/2608